On the Sandy Beach

RASPBERRY RIDGE
BOOK ONE

JESSIE GUSSMAN

Contents

Acknowledgments

Cover art by Julia Gussman
Editing by Heather Hayden
Narration by Jay Dyess
Author Services by CE Author Assistant

Listen to the unabridged audio for FREE performed by Jay Dyess on the Say with Jay channel on YouTube. Get early access to all of Jay's recordings and listen to Jessie's books before they're available to the general public, plus get daily Bible readings by Jay and bonus scenes by becoming a Say with Jay channel member.

One

"Life is not always easy," Vera Miller began, looking out over the crowd of people in front of her. "In fact, sometimes it's downright hard." That was not profound. Everyone who had lived a little knew it. "But life is so much easier if you have the Lord to guide you and help you and hold your hand." She took a deep breath. "And I hope this garden will help everyone who enters its borders to think about their Creator and His love for them, and that contemplation will help them rest in Him."

There were cheers and claps from the crowd as Vera stood at the podium, smiling and hoping that smile reached her eyes.

The overwhelming sadness that seemed to be a part of her life since she had lost her son felt especially heavy today. She wasn't sure why; today was a day of celebration. The garden that she had designed for inner-city Cleveland was now complete and open to the public.

The *Cleveland News and Review* had run a front-cover feature article on her garden designs, lavishly heaping praise upon her for the various gardens she'd designed all over the United States and including quote after quote of people who had been in those gardens and had felt the healing powers within.

God created nature to rejuvenate and renew and refresh humans.

Vera believed that with her whole soul, and that was the foundation that she used in order to create her designs.

"Thank you so much, Vera. We're honored that you not only were able to design our humble city's garden, but that you were able to be here on our opening day celebration." Sadie Lang, member of the Cleveland City Council, spoke into the microphone, her eyes glowing as she looked at Vera, and Vera wasn't quite sure, but it almost looked like she was about ready to cry.

Vera didn't understand how everyone could love her design so much and she could be having so much professional success, when it felt like her personal life was smoldering in ashes behind her.

"It was my pleasure. This is one of my favorite garden designs, and I'm thrilled that everyone seems to be relating to it."

Several more people stepped around to congratulate her as she backed away from the microphone. Someone else began to talk, and she stood in a group of people, listening to them discussing how she always came in under budget and with the design more beautiful than people imagined.

It was true that she always came in under budget. It was one of her goals. And delivering more than what she had promised was another one of her goals.

Maybe she was a little bit of an overachiever. Only children had a tendency to be that way. The fact that her parents had been older and had instilled traditional values in her before they passed probably accounted for it, too.

Except, in her marriage, she hadn't overachieved anything. In fact, she wasn't sure that achieve was even a word that she could use to describe what she had done in her marriage.

Of course, since Trent had passed away, things had been more than strained between Dominic and her.

This could very well be the last project they did together.

Dominic had not been able to attend the opening ceremony, even though his landscaping company had done the work of building her design and making it beautifully real. He had been needed on another project he was working on.

When she designed a garden, Dominic had always put it in. He could do anything she dreamed up, and while she specialized in healing gardens, she'd done other designs, especially in her earlier days of getting established.

Regardless, whatever she designed, Dominic did.

Perhaps Dominic could have made it to today's grand opening.

But he had chosen not to.

"Are you flying home today? Or do you have another project that needs your attention?" The lady, Vera forgot her name and her name tag was underneath the lapel of her jacket, asked as Vera looked around, hoping she would be able to leave soon but knowing she still had the typical meet and greet to do.

The meet and greet was essential for her business, because it was often when she got asked to do another project. The dignitaries and other city leaders that were often at these things would hear about her, take her name back to their various city councils, and suggest that they get her to do their project.

She wasn't going to downplay how important it was for her to do this, but she had to admit, her heart was not in it today, nor had it been for a while.

Losing a child wasn't supposed to do that to a person, although she knew she wasn't going to bounce back immediately. But it had been eighteen months since Trent had passed away.

Eighteen months of slowly growing apart from her husband. Eighteen months of her turning her back on the Lord, despite her job of designing healing gardens and despite the speech she had given today, which echoed the speeches she typically gave.

She still gave lip service to the Lord, but her heart was far from Him.

Maybe there was still a little anger because He had taken her son from her. Even though she knew that she would see Trent again someday. Still, that was hard to balance with the fact that he was no longer on this earth with her. That she wasn't going to have the opportunity to raise him, she would never touch his silky soft hair after she had tucked him in bed, brushing over his forehead and having him say, "Mom. I'm too big for that."

So many things she would never get to do again.

She knew God was good, God was fair, God was loving, kind, and merciful, and she also knew that He worked everything out for her good and His glory, but her son? Did He really have to take her son?

Now her marriage. She was going to lose it, too, she was sure.

Why else would Dominic not be here?

"You did an awesome job as always," Peggy Cole, her best friend, said as she wrapped an arm around Vera and came alongside her.

They walked a little way away from the crowd and the celebration, and Vera allowed herself to sag a little in Peggy's warm embrace.

"Thank you for being here. I appreciate seeing a familiar face and having a friend."

Peggy had grown up in Raspberry Ridge, Michigan, along with Vera. But life had taken Peggy away, although it had been very generous to her in material goods, and Peggy could afford to take a day off from her regularly scheduled pedicures and manicures and facials and massages, and fly to Cleveland to support her friend.

"You know all you have to do is ask. I might have come even if you hadn't asked. There's something fun about Cleveland, with Lake Erie so close. It's a little like being back home."

"I tried to reflect that in the garden. There are several little bridge walkways over shallow water underneath. It seemed very Cleveland-ish."

"You always have a way of drawing in the topography of the area you're designing, while still making each design fresh and new and interesting. Not to mention, soothing. I think this might be your best design yet."

Peggy was not the first person to tell her that, and Vera couldn't disagree. She felt like she was growing in her ability to design.

"It seems like the more depressed I get, the better I'm able to design."

"I think some of the greatest works of art ever made were made out of times of great trial or distress. Possibly Beethoven's greatest symphony was written when he couldn't hear a note of it."

"This is correct, but it makes for a not very fun time for the designer/creator."

"I really wish you'd see someone. A counselor, even if it's just your church pastor or his wife."

She didn't mention to Peggy that she hadn't been to church since the one in Raspberry Ridge had closed several years ago. Up until that point, she'd been very involved in church. She wanted her son to grow up with a strong knowledge of the Bible and a strong basis of the character and integrity that living for the Lord entailed.

But the church had closed, and six months later, her son was gone.

"You haven't found a church yet, have you?"

"Raspberry Ridge is pretty small. There aren't a whole lot of churches to choose from, since the only one in town is closed down."

"Strawberry Sands isn't that far away, and neither is Blueberry Beach. Either one has good churches. I know, because I've been to both of them and so have you. In fact, we sang at those churches, with Dominic accompanying us on his guitar."

At the mention of Dominic, Vera looked away.

"Vera. You can fix this. He adores you."

"And I love him." She pursed her lips and looked out over the garden. "Do you remember that story in the Bible about the rich man who died and went to hell, and how he talked to Abraham and asked Abraham if Abraham could dip his fingers in cold water and just touch his tongue with them, and Abraham said there's too great a chasm between us for me to be able to get to you?"

"I remember," Peggy said solemnly.

"That's how I feel things are between Dominic and me. We can talk to each other. We have. We created this garden together. I had some ideas for the bridges, and I had to tweak them a little so he was able to make them, and a few other things. We...still work well together, but there's this chasm between us."

"And it's not like the chasm in the Bible. You can cross it. It's just going to take...effort."

She didn't know whether she agreed with Peggy or not. It felt like Dominic wasn't very interested. He seemed so busy and uninterested. Very different from the way he'd been when they had been dating and married for the first few years or so. Then after their son came, they both doted on him and had been thrilled that God had given them a child in their thirties.

Now, she was over forty, and all hope of having a child was pretty much gone. She hadn't quite hit the big M, but it was looming, she could feel it, and it hardly mattered, since she and her husband had barely touched since Trent's funeral.

"You know, I think it all started with Trent."

"You can't blame my son," she said, more defensive than she would have expected herself to be. Especially with her best friend, whom she knew only wanted the best for her.

"I'm not blaming him. I'm just saying, things were really good between you and Dominic until Trent passed away. Maybe...maybe you need a healing garden of your own."

Vera found herself very resistant to that idea, even though part of her felt like Peggy might have been on to something. "Like I have time to do that. And where would I do it anyway? In Raspberry Ridge next to our house? I hardly think so."

"There's that area of ground right there at the end of the road at the bluffs on the western side of town. Where you take the trail to go to the bluffs and down to the stone beach where there are those few beach houses and where Garrett Irving has his fishing business. It's all grown up in weeds and looks nasty. Remember how we used to say we should plant flowers there, and actually for a couple of years, we did. Even just a few little colorful blooms made it seem not so shaggy and ugly."

"I know where you mean. Having something there would be a nice addition to Raspberry Ridge." That's where she'd raised her son. She had not exactly semiretired, but she had taken a bit of a break since Trent passed, not designing anything except this garden.

Back when Trent had been alive, she had taken him with her every place she went, and she didn't go if he couldn't. Dominic had gone as well, and they had talked about things together. That's how they worked best, discussing things, she on the design side, he on the actual practical side. Sometimes she got a little carried away with what could be accomplished, and Dominic knew her goals, to always come in under budget and always over deliver.

She'd never worked with anyone as well as she worked with Dominic.

"Think about it. It might actually be good for you. Healing, you know." Peggy squeezed her arm, and just then, several ladies came over, complimenting her on her design and telling them that they'd already enjoyed spending time in the garden.

Peggy's arm slid from her shoulders, although Peggy stayed near her. She knew that when Dominic wasn't around, Vera especially appreciated her presence. It was hard to mingle with strangers, especially in the last eighteen months. It used to be she would come to these things and leave smiling because she turned strangers into friends. But nowadays, their faces just blended together and she left as soon as she was able to, unable to dredge up the interest that she should show in other people or to have the energy to invest in their lives and start building friendships.

Peggy's words hung in the back of her head though, and on the flight home to Raspberry Ridge, she leaned her head back in the airplane, wondering if maybe Peggy was onto something. Her friend was wise, and her advice had never steered wrong. After all, Peggy was the one who suggested that she accept Dominic's offer of a date, and that first date had been the last time she'd ever thought about another man. Dominic was all she wanted.

Two

Dominic took a hammer and pounded in the stake in front of him. He had marked all the places where they were planting pine trees with big orange painted Xs, but he still used a measuring tape to make sure that he was getting the exact correct distance between trees.

He finished pounding the stake again and measured the distance to the next, making sure he was exactly on the line before he put the stake where the tree was supposed to go and pounded it in.

Part of the reason why his work was so in demand was because of the precision that he demanded from himself and from his employees.

That precision had reached a new level after Trent had passed away. He had thrown himself into his work, as he supposed was common for men to do. It gave him something to keep his mind active, and he didn't ruminate over the fact that the boy that he had expected to spend his life working beside wouldn't run his company with him, nor would he eventually pass it over to him.

In fact, the next time he would see him would be in heaven, when Dominic entered the pearly gates.

That thought itself was sobering enough that he shoved it aside and squinted at his measuring tape, making sure it was exactly right. He took the stake and carefully positioned it in the precise location, holding it with a steady hand, and grabbing the hammer back out of his belt, he pounded it in.

He wouldn't trust any of his workers to do this job. They could put the trees in, because he could assume that they could take a stake out and point the tip of the hole digger right in the hole that the stake came out of.

That didn't take too much self-control or precision. Although, anyone who was sloppy in their job found a new job.

Which meant his turnover should be high, except he paid his workers exceptionally well, because he could afford to. His reputation had gone far beyond the little corner of Michigan where he'd grown up beside the lake, and while he found his first major success in Chicago, he'd done landscaping all over the country.

His early success was thanks to his wife, Vera, who refused to allow anyone except for him to do her designs.

And once he met her, he did no landscaping for any other designer, other than his wife.

Then once Trent died, he had to keep himself busy, and he'd taken extra jobs, pushing himself far harder than he probably should, considering that he didn't have the energy or stamina that he had in his twenties. He was in his early forties, and he felt it at night, after he'd sat down for five minutes. Then his body stiffened up, and his joints and muscles ached with a pain that seemed to soak into his bones.

Maybe that was when it hit hardest, the knowledge that his son was truly gone forever.

Or maybe it was the knowledge that he had pretty much self-destructed his marriage.

He knew that a marriage couldn't thrive if the couple didn't put any time or effort into it, and since his son had passed, Vera's sadness on top of his own was way more than he could handle. Maybe that was why he had started taking the extra jobs, to get himself away from her, so he didn't have to see her suffering.

It was hard to see the person a man loved more than anything else in the world suffering the way his wife had.

She had loved their son just as much, maybe more, than he had. And Trent's death had devastated her.

Perhaps because she blamed herself, but he was probably more to blame. He hadn't been there.

Not at first.

And he had downplayed her concerns when she had first voiced them to him. The cough, fever, lethargy, she'd called him to ask what she should do, and Dominic told her that kids got sick, they laid around until they felt better, don't worry about it.

He'd been finishing up her latest design in Texas and hadn't wanted to fly home. How many times in the eighteen months since had he wished that he had heard the extra note of concern in Vera's voice, paid attention to it, and dropped everything to go home to her?

How many times had he wished he said, "It's probably nothing, but if you're truly concerned about it, go to the ER."

Trent had plenty of colds before. And he'd always done exactly what Dominic said, laid around until he felt better. Once he felt better, he was back up and running around.

He didn't realize that this time was different. Vera had, but like she usually did, she wanted his input. She didn't want to make the decision alone, she wanted the other parent, the other half of Trent, the other half of her, the one she depended on to walk with her through life, she wanted him, Dominic, to help her in her decision.

His reassurance had made her hesitate, and she hadn't called an ambulance for Trent for another four hours.

Perhaps the meningitis could have been stopped and their son saved had she taken him immediately.

Of course, that was all conjecture at this point in time, Dominic thought as he pounded another stake in, possibly hitting it harder than he needed to as the top knuckled down and one small corner split off.

He'd let Vera down. He'd let Trent down. He had been the protector and provider for his family, and he'd been the one who broke the family apart.

Then, he couldn't stand to see his wife's guilt and grief, but had kept himself busy, focusing on trying to make himself better. After all, didn't the experts say that you can't help anyone until you help yourself?

Maybe that was true in an airplane when he needed to put his oxygen mask on first, but it wasn't true in a marriage. Not even a little bit. It was a lie from the devil, and the Bible did not support it. Not with one single verse.

He knew that now, of course. But at the time, he was just trying to get away from the pain.

Now, things had gotten so bad, he didn't know what to do to fix them. Anything he tried to do would be met with cool indifference by his wife. It was just easier to stay away.

Of course, in his life, he hadn't typically chosen the easier route.

"Hey, Boss. When you get a minute, I need you to come over here and check on the placement of the flowers. I've got them marked out, but I just wanted to have your eye on it before I started putting the bulbs in."

"All right. I'll be right over, as soon as I finish these last four stakes."

Ricky turned and went back toward the area where he'd been working, and Dominic determined that he would focus on his job and stop ruminating over the things he should have done better. They were in the past, and he couldn't fix them. Just like he most likely couldn't fix his marriage.

Vera had designed one garden since their son had passed. The Cleveland garden opened a week or so ago, and as far as he knew, she didn't have anything else lined up, not for him to do anyway. They hadn't exactly been communicating excessively, but it was their latest project, and something told him it would be their last project together.

That thought made him sad all over again, and he felt like mourning, not as bad as when his son had died, but definitely mourning the loss of something beautiful. Because their marriage had been a beautiful thing. Definitely the picture of Christ and the church which it was supposed to be. He didn't know another marriage that reflected it the way Vera and his had.

But it hadn't been easy. They both worked hard to make that happen.

He shoved his hammer in his tool belt, after pounding the last four stakes in, and took one step toward Ricky before his phone buzzed in his pocket.

While he was working, he never pulled his phone out, but since he was walking from one spot to another, he could probably check. He had put bids out on several different projects, and he also was awaiting the go-ahead from four more. All those needed was approval of the budget from the city council in charge, and he would be starting. He didn't know which one would be first, and he wasn't sure he could get all four of them done. But at least he was staying busy. That was the important thing.

Pulling his phone out, he glanced at the area where he'd be walking, saw that there were no obstacles he could run into, and looked down at his phone.

He stopped abruptly. An email had just come in from his wife.

Three

Vera hadn't spoken with Dominic in days. When they happened to be home at the same time, they passed through the halls in the house like ghosts who were unable to speak.

She didn't cook, and he didn't complain about it. He didn't expect her to do anything with him, and she did the same. She had taken on some designing jobs, but they were small, inner-city rooftop garden designs, an area that she'd been slightly curious about, and she had wanted to stretch her wings a little. It seemed like a good change from the gardens that she had been designing, and truth be told, it kept her from interacting with Dominic, which felt more and more awkward.

They still shared a room, but she lay curled on her side of the bed, and she didn't know what he did on his, but she did know he didn't touch her.

Which was just fine with her.

It made sense that part of their relationship died along with everything else. And while she mourned it, she accepted the demise as inevitable. The way she had their relationship. The way she had her depression.

But after spending a week thinking about what Peggy had said, she decided that she would take this to the Lord in prayer.

She used to do it all the time, but she'd gotten away from Him, feeling a little bit like God had double-crossed her. He'd given her the son she'd always wanted, and then He'd taken him away.

But she still didn't doubt that there was a God, and she knew, even if she didn't feel, that He was good. She also knew there was only one way to heaven, and a life spent living for anything other than the Lord was completely wasted, because her rewards in eternity would be based on what she did in this life. That was all documented in the Bible, and she believed it.

She just...hadn't been able to get through the fog of grief in order to live it.

So, she'd taken the idea of designing and building a healing garden here in Raspberry Ridge to the Lord.

She'd only prayed one time before she had the feeling settle on her, a feeling that she had more than once in her life, when something was exactly right. It was the feeling she had on her first date with Dominic. It was the feeling she had when a design came together perfectly. And it was the feeling she had when she prayed about whether or not she should design a healing garden and ask Dominic to build it with her.

She had made a bargain with the Lord, which she had always thought was foolish. A person should not bargain with the Lord. Who was she, made out of dust, small and insignificant in the vastness of creation, to attempt to bargain with the One who made it all?

But bargain she did. She told the Lord that fine, she'd design the garden, if Dominic would agree to build it.

She'd never worked with another landscaper, and she never intended to, no matter what Dominic did. They hadn't ever said to each other, "we'll never work with anyone but each other," but it had been a theme throughout their marriage. And maybe part of the reason their marriage had been so good. Regardless, her best work was done when Dominic was a part of it. And if she was going to make a healing garden in memory of her son, it would be her best work. She would be sure of it.

So, knowing it was what she was supposed to do, she took a few days to try to figure out how to contact her husband.

By text? That seemed kind of personal, and she didn't really have that kind of relationship with him anymore. Email felt a little distant, but much safer. And professional. She wanted him to help her design and build a garden in Raspberry Ridge. That was definitely email worthy.

She could message him. Through one of the social media apps. But that...never made her comfortable. She didn't enjoy using them, and neither one of them were on social media for personal purposes. They posted pictures of their gardens, their designs, their work in progress. They didn't post personal pictures, and not once had they spoken about their son on any social media platform.

In the end, she went with the email.

Before Trent passed away, she would have texted without thinking about it, but now she put together the most professional email she could. Professional and persuasive, because as she'd been praying about the idea, she'd fallen in love with it, already had ideas in her head, but she knew that it could not be completed without Dominic's agreement.

Good afternoon,

I hope you're well, I know it's been a while since we've spoken. The grand opening in Cleveland went well, and they said it was probably some of my best work. Of course, everyone knows that you are the one who brings my work to life, and so I owe you a debt of gratitude for taking the design I put on paper and making it beautiful in real life.

I'm writing today though, because I had an idea while I was at the grand opening in Cleveland, and while I was resistant at first, I think it might be a good idea.

I know we haven't been close since Trent died, and I assume that any day you're going to...want a divorce.

Before that happens, I thought we could team up for one last project. A healing garden in Raspberry Ridge in memory of Trent.

Like I said, I have some ideas, but it won't be a small project. It will mean at least a week or more of work. I am willing to help. Especially because I know you weren't expecting a project this large at this time.

I'm not going to do the project if you are not on board with it.

Since we were married, I've never designed a project and worked with anyone but you to complete it. I know it hasn't been the same with you, and I maybe understand a little of why. Regardless, I'm asking for one last project together. For our son.

If you're interested, I'll be at our home in Raspberry Ridge for the next two months. After that, I'm planning a trip to Europe.

If you'd like to meet to discuss it, fly home. I have some of the sketches ready, and I'm working on more.

Sincerely,

Vera

Four

Dominic stared at his phone. Divorce? She thought he was considering divorce?

He hadn't even allowed himself to think that word, but he could understand why she might think he was contemplating it.

She hit him below the belt so to speak, with what she had said about him working with other designers. They had had an unspoken agreement that they would only work with each other. It was the safest way to conduct a marriage. And it had been more than profitable for both of them. It kept their work in high demand. If someone wanted him, they had to have her too. And vice versa. Which had precipitated his rise to fame.

She had been more popular than he when they had gotten together, since landscapers didn't typically travel for jobs outside a certain area. But Vera had refused to work with anyone but him, and his popularity had grown because of that. It was the one thing that had made his career take off, and in the last year, his income had eclipsed hers for the first time.

Not that they had ever been competitive in that area at all.

On the contrary, he had always been her biggest fan, and he couldn't imagine anyone who could support him better than what she had.

Still, his star was definitely on the rise, although that had nothing to do with his frenetic work pace.

In fact, if anything, he would want to slow down some, spend time with his family, except... It felt lonely and cold in the house without Trent running through the rooms, laughing and begging him to stop for a few moments to see his latest project or to play with him.

Coming home had become a haven, until it wasn't.

But this garden that she wanted...

He couldn't tell Vera no.

So he would make room in his schedule, whatever that meant. Even if it meant the unthinkable, that he wouldn't be there to oversee his current project and his crew had to do it by themselves.

Except she did mention divorce. She said it almost like she expected it was going to happen. That hadn't been in his vocabulary at all, but... he supposed that was the natural ending, since they didn't really talk anymore. He couldn't remember the last time he touched her, and he couldn't even remember the last time they'd sat at the table in the kitchen and eaten together.

When he was home, he grabbed a sandwich or something and sat in front of the TV or went into his study and worked.

He didn't know what she did. He just couldn't stand to see the sadness in her eyes, the depression that almost followed her around like a black cloud, and the quiet, unnatural stillness of their house.

But he would deal with it for the time it took to make this garden.

Pulling up an airline website on his phone, he looked to see the soonest he could get tickets to Ann Arbor. That's where he parked his car, where he flew in and out of. It was the closest airport to their house and the one they always used.

Once he got his ticket, he hit reply and sent one sentence back to his wife.

I'll be home tomorrow.

Five

era paced from one end of the dining room to the other.

Dominic was coming today.

She didn't know why that made her nervous. It wasn't like they hadn't been married for over ten years.

She stopped at the table and adjusted the flowers that sat in the vase in the middle of it. They were flowers that she had gone out this morning and cut from their own yard. She typically did that when she was home and there were flowers blooming.

She had designed their yard so there would always be flowers, from the earliest time in the spring until the mums bloomed in late fall.

Feeling a little more settled as she arranged the flowers so they looked perfect, she stood back, taking a deep breath and telling herself that it was just her husband. That was all.

It wasn't like she hadn't seen him, hadn't brushed by him in the hall, or in the kitchen or even in the yard, multiple times in the last few months, even if they hadn't shared any deep, meaningful conversations.

When they first got together, talking hadn't necessarily been his thing. He was okay with talking about work, talking about landscaping making her designs come to life, or talking about facts and even opinions.

But the deeper things that she liked to know, how he was feeling, what his thoughts were, his plans and hopes and dreams, and sharing hers, hadn't come easily to him.

She supposed it was a male thing, but he'd made the effort because he knew that was what it took for her to feel connected to him.

They bumped along and finally figured out how to speak each other's love language.

His was touch, and she had taken to brushing his shoulders with her fingers when she walked by him, running her hand down his arm, coming over and putting her arm around him for no reason, or on quiet evenings together, she gave him foot massages and rubbed his back and shoulders after a particularly long, hard day at work.

She had thought their marriage was indestructible, but she remembered what the Bible said about pride going before fall.

Her phone rang, making her jump. Half expecting it to be her husband, she couldn't deny that there was a little pang of disappointment that went through her when she saw that it was her friend, Peggy.

"Hello?"

"Vera. I'm thinking about you."

She hadn't talked to Peggy since they'd seen each other over a week ago in Cleveland.

"I got your text that you got safely back to California, and I'm here in Michigan. Nothing much going on." Except her husband was coming home today, and they had an appointment to talk.

Not an appointment. All he said was *I'll be home tomorrow*. He might not even arrive until late.

"I was really getting excited about the idea of the healing garden. I took the liberty of getting some inspiration from the Internet, and I put it together in an email. But I wanted to call and chat with you first before I sent it. You know, something like that coming out of the blue, it might be a little pushy. You know I would have meant the very best, but...it's always nice to send it with a few words."

"Thank you. You're right. Whatever you sent, I would assume you had the very best intentions for it. I am eager to look at your designs." She paused, fingering the edge of the table, running her fingernail along a corner, before tapping it on the polished wood. "I decided I was going to do what you suggested."

"Really? You're making a healing garden in memory of Trent?"

She flinched a little at the mention of his name, glad that Peggy couldn't see. Peggy was always super sensitive to her feelings, and Vera had often insisted that she would prefer people talk about Trent, rather than acting like he had never been born. It seemed like a waste of the years to not acknowledge that he had walked the earth, just because it caused her a little sliver of pain. All right, a big hit of pain, every time someone said his name, but that didn't mean that she didn't like hearing it. It just hurt too.

There were plenty of things that hurt and felt good at the same time.

"Yes. You have never given me bad advice, and I assumed that this time was no different. I decided that it was silly of me to not pay attention."

"I appreciate that. You know I have your best interest at heart." Peggy's voice was cheerful, but then she spoke in a more sober tone. "Can I give you one more piece of advice?"

"Sure. Shoot," Vera said, looking around the room and walking over to a picture frame that she adjusted a fraction of an inch, to make it exactly straight.

"You and Dominic had something really special. It's something that only comes around once in a lifetime, and not for everyone. It's worth whatever effort you have to put in to get it back."

"Sometimes, you can't get the water that flowed under the bridge back."

"You still have the bridge. And there is still water flowing. You have to let bygones be bygones and allow what you go through to make you stronger, not...tear down the bridge because there was a problem with the water."

She wasn't sure whether those analogies were on target or not, but she appreciated her friend.

"I'll keep that in mind." She wanted to remind Peggy that it took two to have a relationship, and Vera wasn't the one who had started working with other people, throwing herself into her work, and neglecting her marriage. She could hardly take care of her marriage when her husband was in another state, working on a project she had nothing to do with.

Of course, lots of people had marriages like that. Not everyone was blessed enough to have a husband with a vocation that was so connected to what she did as a vocation. Those other people somehow made it work. Surely Vera could too. Even if Dominic wanted to continue to go in whatever direction he was going in.

It was lucrative anyway.

They chatted a bit more, then hung up.

Vera decided that she could work on some of her designs, that time would fly past faster when she lost herself in them. That's the way it was, she could lose herself for hours in her designs.

She just wanted to be alert and know exactly when Dominic showed up. She didn't want to be caught unawares and unprepared.

Regardless, it could be late until he arrived, since he hadn't said what time. So, taking one last look around the dining room to make sure she had left everything in a perfect position, she walked through the house to the sunroom, which she used as her office.

As she thought, she soon got lost in her designs, and time flew by. The next thing she knew, her stomach was growling and it was starting to get dark outside.

Still, she had most of the designs ready, only a few little things that she had gotten stuck on.

Knowing they would work themselves out if she allowed the thoughts to percolate in the back of her head, she glanced at the time.

Eight o'clock. Well, he had four hours to make good on his word.

That was a rather negative thought, and she tried not to focus on it. After all, Dominic had always been a man of his word. She hadn't had to wonder whether or not he was going to do what he said he was going to do. If it was humanly possible, he would keep his word.

That was then. She honestly wasn't sure what kind of man he had turned into over the last eighteen months. She most definitely was not the same woman.

After making herself a sandwich, and only eating half of it, and downing an entire glass of water, she had only killed twelve minutes.

Carefully disposing of the other half of the sandwich, and washing her dishes, drying them, and putting them away, she looked around the kitchen.

Pristine.

When Trent had been alive, Dominic had come and spoken with her about the standards she had for cleanliness.

She knew they were rather high, and he had jokingly said to her that maybe she should try letting a dish sit on the counter, just to get herself used to a bit of a mess. Not that one dish was a mess.

But the underlying premise behind his words had been correct. She needed to relax. And she had. She allowed Trent to keep his toys out on the floor all day long, without telling him to pick them up and put them away. Which she had been tempted to do, just because she was constantly arranging things, making them better, picking things up, and making them perfect.

For some reason, that thought led to another, and soon her feet had moved from the kitchen, down the hallway, and before she knew it, her hand rested on the doorknob of the second door to the right. It was the one directly across the hall from the master bedroom. It had been Trent's room for his entire eight years on this earth.

She hadn't changed a thing about his room, from the way it was the day he died, other than to make the bed.

She had been in such a rush to get him out of bed and into the ambulance, she hadn't made the bed, which was...huge for her.

Pushing her memories of that day aside, she twisted the doorknob and cracked the door.

He had been sick the last day and a half of his life, and she had spent a lot of time by his bedside, getting up and down, getting him a drink, getting him anything that she thought he might eat, taking his temperature religiously, and even documenting it in a notebook.

In her spare time, she'd gone around, picking up everything off the floor, putting it all neatly away.

His teddy bear, which he was too mature for, except for times when he was tired or ill, still sat on his bed, right by the pillow.

She'd almost put the bear in the casket.

But she hadn't been able to bring herself to come into the room after his death. His favorite T-shirt and scruffy pair of jeans had been in the laundry, and she hadn't had to go in to get clothes to take to the funeral home.

She had wanted to dress him in a suit and tie, his Easter outfit that year, but Dominic had gently suggested that perhaps they should dress him in the clothes that he would have chosen to wear himself.

Vera could hardly argue with that. Trent had kept his tie on long enough for her to take Easter pictures before they left for church that morning, but it had been stuffed in his pocket after two minutes in the car.

She had made him put it back on, so Gertie could take pictures of her family standing on the church steps. And one with Lake Michigan at their back. It was probably her favorite picture of their family, even though it wasn't a perfect picture.

It hung on the wall of their bedroom.

The wind was blowing, and her hair was blown partially over her face. Dominic had said something funny, something to make everyone laugh so that they were smiling for the pictures, only it was a little bit off color, suggestive, something only she would pick up on. A personal joke. She had looked at him, laughter in her gaze, as he stared at the camera, his jaw tilted up in what might have been an arrogant direction, but she knew better. Just competent, but never, ever arrogant.

Trent had giggled, totally missing the deeper part of the joke, and the lake was a deep, brilliant blue behind them, with a light blue sky with puffy clouds dotting it, a perfect picture. Perfect picture of a perfect family.

She had looked at that picture every night since she hung it in their room and thought about how blessed she was, what a perfect family she had.

Of course, that had been until the Lord had taken Trent away, just a few short months later.

She didn't walk into the room, just looked. Maybe the pain was slightly more dull than it had been, but it was so heavy, so strong that she couldn't do anything more than just sweep her eyes around the room and pull the door closed. Wanting to cry, she turned and almost ran headlong into her husband.

"Whoa. Sorry," he said, grabbing her shoulders to make sure she didn't fall and holding on just long enough to make sure she was steady before he dropped his hands.

"I'm sorry. I didn't hear you come home."

"I got the earliest tickets I could, but traffic was terrible in Ann Arbor, and I got held up for over an hour. You know how it can be when you hit rush hour and there's an accident."

"Yeah. Sorry about that."

She'd been there. She knew how it was. And understood that he was coming home as quickly as possible. She appreciated it. But she wasn't sure exactly what that meant.

She almost hadn't put the D word in her email. But she figured she might as well take the bull by the horns and face things. Maybe she had been burying things too long.

"It's not your fault."

They stood there, staring awkwardly first at each other, then looking away. Neither one of them seemed to know what to say.

He shifted on his feet; she kept her feet planted, her arms at her sides. She did not fidget. At least, she tried not to. She had been known to pace, but her default when she was nervous was to straighten things up.

There was nothing in the hall to straighten, other than the man in front of her, but he was already...perfect.

Six

Vera let her eyes track to the stubble on Dominic's jaw. She always thought that was so sexy, the way he looked after he worked all day, and it looked like he hadn't shaved last night either. Maybe working late so he could leave early today to be home.

She didn't know what kind of inconvenience it was for him to be here.

His hands, brown and capable, shifted at his sides before he finally put one in his pocket and hooked another behind his neck. That was a sure way to tell that he was uneasy.

Her presence did not used to make him uneasy.

"Have you eaten? Would you like to go to the kitchen and grab a sandwich and we can sit at the dining room table and talk? I can get my computer and show you my thoughts."

"Sure, that'll be fine. But I'm pretty busy. Are you sure it's something you really want to do? I mean, I haven't been here for very long, but it looked to me like you couldn't even walk in his room."

She'd forgotten. After Trent passed away, Dominic had spent hours on his knees beside Trent's bed, praying for she didn't know what. It was too late to bring her son back.

"Yes. I'm sure."

Until that point, she honestly hadn't been, although the designs had gone together, at least most of them, so easily that she knew she was doing the right thing.

She had had confirmation from the Lord, but she didn't say that to Dominic as she walked past him, carefully, without touching him, and moved to the kitchen. Pulling out the ham rather than the turkey breast, because that was his preference, along with mustard. She preferred mayonnaise.

He got the sourdough bread out, which was the one thing they both agreed on when they were making a sandwich.

She left the onions and the lettuce in the refrigerator because Dominic preferred not to have them on his sandwich, although he would eat it with them if he had to.

There was a little bit of Swiss cheese left, and she pulled that out as well. He had gotten the two slices of bread out and put them on a plate. She arranged the ham neatly, folding it over and making it look artistic, even though it was just a sandwich that was going to be gone in the next ten minutes. Five, if Dominic was really hungry.

He squirted mustard on the piece of bread that was on his side, while she put one and a half slices of Swiss cheese on. The first slice, she set over the entire sandwich, the second slice she broke in half and put diagonally across.

She had made it that way one time years ago as a joke, and he had said that it was his favorite sandwich that he had ever eaten, mostly because of the surprise places where he got a little bit of extra cheese.

It was something little they'd done years ago, and ever after, every sandwich she ever made him was exactly that way. One slice of cheese over the whole sandwich, and one half slice diagonally.

He put the mustard away while she sealed up the cheese and ham and then waited for him to be done in the refrigerator before she walked around and put them back in while he closed the sandwich and grabbed a glass. She was already in the freezer to get ice out of the ice cube trays.

The ice dispenser had broken in the refrigerator shortly before Trent had passed away. She remembered it, because when his fever had spiked to 103, she had panicked and put ice in baggies, holding it next to his throat while she called 911.

She had to reach into the ice cube tray to get the ice out.

She had three cubes in her hand, and Dominic was waiting with a glass when she turned. She allowed them to clink into it one at a time before she moved away and he filled his glass the rest of the way up with water.

She walked to the sunroom, which doubled as her office, grabbing her computer and walking back to the dining room where Dominic was already settled at the table.

Before Trent came, this would be cozy, a normal night for them. Except for the silence between them. Even after Trent came, there were plenty of evenings after he went to bed where they worked together at the table. She with her designs, him working on purchase orders, scheduling, and payroll.

He had a lot more to do with his business than she did, and occasionally she helped him. Particularly when he was knee-deep in a job. When it was her knee-deep in designs, he helped around the house, taking care of Trent and cooking, although Dominic's main claim to fame was the special chicken he made that was his dad's recipe.

Not that she ever minded. She just appreciated having the burden taken off her shoulders. Having someone who knew her so well they knew exactly what would help and what they needed to do in order to ease her burden.

"What gave you this idea?" Dominic asked as she sat down, his sandwich untouched.

"Peggy. She suggested it."

"When did you see Peggy?" he asked, taking a deep drink of his water.

"In Cleveland, at the grand opening of the inner-city healing garden we created together."

He jerked his head, and then he said, "I'll pray."

They bowed their heads together, and it was the first time they prayed together since Trent's funeral.

She supposed she kept track of that because prayer had always been an important part of her life, but it had been even more important in Dominic's life. He hadn't had the best upbringing, and he always said it was because of his prayers, lying in bed at night, wherever he happened to be sleeping, that God would help him make a family that wasn't like the ones that he'd grown up in.

That enabled him to rise above his circumstances and have a life that was more than welfare dependence and cigarettes and alcohol for fun.

She couldn't even imagine Dominic as that kind of person, although he was most definitely a blue-collar worker. People didn't have to look very hard to see that about him. Since he was out in the sun all summer long, and he was brown, the whole way to his shirt collar and both arms.

With his T-shirt off, he looked a little funny, with tan lines clearly marked around his neck and arms, but she loved that about him. Loved what that said about his work ethic, about his standards, about his convictions and character.

He laughed at himself more than once, but she never had. It represented everything she loved about him.

"I'll be done with this in a sec, but I can watch if you want to start showing me."

"Well, first, Peggy suggested we do it in memory of…Trent." She forced his name out. She could count on one hand the number of times she'd said his name since he died, even though she told people she didn't want them to be afraid to say it or to push him under the rug like he had never been born.

"And that's why I was standing in his bedroom. Thinking about the things he loved, and thinking about how we can honor him and still make it a calming place for anyone going through any kind of trauma or heartbreak."

Including divorce.

She did not utter those words, but she thought that maybe the Lord was having them design this garden because she was going to need it.

That's why she had decided on the European vacation, or at least had it ready to book. She thought she was going to need it. But she just hadn't quite been able to push the buy button.

Castles and mountains and churches and beautiful, picturesque countrysides surely would heal her heart, although maybe not as good as the garden that she had created in her head to honor Trent.

"He loved the water. And I wanted to have a water fountain in the middle of it. Not at the edge where everyone can see it, but where you have to walk deeper in. It would be the heart of the garden. With benches around," she said, and she brought up the first design. It was the water fountain. Which was more like a stream, coming down out of the rocks. It split into two streams, one going to a waterfall, and one curving around, slower and more peaceful. It would not be easy to build. Dominic had done several of them, but none exactly like this one.

His mouth flattened, but he nodded, his eyes intelligent and thoughtful as he looked at it. "That's doable. That'll look good too. I know exactly what kind of stone I can use. Depending what color flowers you're going to have, a gray sandstone would be perfect."

"I thought a little darker stone, a brown, to match the color of the beach down below the bluffs."

"Trent's favorite beach was the sandy beach down by Blueberry Beach. That's where he loved going best."

She closed her mouth. He didn't too often argue with her or even suggest any improvements on her design, but he was right about that. The darker color she had wanted wasn't going to look as good, but she had done it in memory of Trent. But the sandy color would be reminiscent of all their times on the sandy beach, which Trent had loved.

"You're right. Let's make that a sandy-colored stone." She made a note on the design, and she knew the images would automatically reconfigure to be exactly what Dominic had suggested.

"I'd like the benches to be comfortable. Not the straight-backed benches that you often find, but a more relaxed design. I know that will be more expensive."

"Yeah. Twice as much," Dominic said thoughtfully before he took another bite of sandwich, holding the last small piece in his hand. He could eat twice as fast as she could, even faster if he was in a hurry.

"But I think it's important. Sometimes people need to spend a little longer, and I want this garden to invite that."

"Got it," he said, the last bite disappearing in his mouth.

He shoved his plate away and chewed for a bit before taking a big drink of his water and setting it over by his plate. She had switched to another design, and he adjusted the computer so he could see the screen better, pulling it a little bit closer.

"This is a picture of the paths that I'd like to have through the garden. Around the fountain will be paved, with pavers, sandstone color, because you're right. That's the better color. I'll have a plethora of flowers, some that bloom in every season, so there will always be something blooming around the fountain. This is how the walkway will look from the gate."

"Did you take the measurements?"

"I went down and measured the area. It's that space that's right at the end of the road, where it dead-ends at the end of Raspberry Ridge Road. The parking lot is off to the left, and the trail to go down to the bluffs is on the right. People would walk across in front of the garden to get to the trail to the bluffs. I marked it off roughly, since the ground was a little hard and I couldn't get my little stakes to go in very well."

He used big wooden stakes usually when he was marking something, but she just had little plastic ones. They were good for soft dirt, but not much else.

"All right. Tomorrow we can go down to get the exact measurements. Make sure this is all going to fit."

If it didn't fit, he would adjust things to make it work. They would work together until he could bring her design to life in a beautiful way. With whatever tweaks were needed.

"I measured the depth as well. We have as much room there as we need to work with, depending on how big we want to make it, and... I have some money set aside, which I was going to put into this. I was hoping you would donate some as well."

She didn't say anything more, and he nodded. "Business has been good, and whatever the cost is, I'll cover it."

They hadn't used to keep their finances separate. But since she had a business and he had a business, their money went into different accounts. She hadn't checked on his account for over a year. Since the last time they paid taxes.

She didn't know whether he knew what was in her accounts or not. But since their home was paid off, they didn't have too many expenses, other than traveling expenses, which were a tax deduction for both of them, and food and utilities.

They were set. They could have traveled the world with Trent if they wanted to.

But now, what was the point? She had a hard time getting excited about going somewhere when it was just going to be her. After planning her trips to get the maximum enjoyment for Trent, they weren't a whole lot of fun when it was just for her own pleasure.

"Any more?" Dominic asked, as she showed him the last of the plans.

Looking at her phone, she could see it was almost ten o'clock. Time flew when they were together. Especially when they were talking about a project they were working on together. She always loved this.

"No. That said, I still have a few other things I'm working on, but they just weren't coming together. That's again why I was in Trent's room."

"All right. If you can send me the specs, I'll see if I can get a supplies list together and put an order in. This will be big enough that I'll just go ahead and have them deliver it. That'll give me a few days to do some measuring and make sure everything's going to work. I might need to rent a bulldozer. We'll see."

"All right."

She tapped a few buttons on her computer, attached his requested specs to an email, and sent it without writing anything.

"I'm going to bed," she said, suddenly overwhelmed and tired. She probably should have modulated her announcement with a "thanks for doing this," or "what are you planning for the rest of the evening?" or something. It felt a little abrupt after it was out of her mouth, but it had been a stressful day.

However, she felt like she needed to face these things in order to move on. She had been stuck in a holding pattern for too long. She didn't want to forget Trent, couldn't ever forget Trent, but she did need to move on with her life. With or without Dominic.

Seven

Dominic lay in bed, staring at the ceiling, which was barely visible in the light of the almost full moon shining in through the window.

If he turned his head, he'd be able to see the moonlight shining on the water of Lake Michigan. That was why he loved this room in this house. It was the view of the lake, the calm and strength that he seemed to draw every time he looked at it. He had felt like Vera and he had made a home here, cozy and intimate, and perfect for raising children.

Then Vera had been unable to get pregnant.

Maybe it was his fault, he didn't know. They hadn't really tried, except it just never happened.

Until it did. And they'd both been over the moon. By that time, they'd been well-established, and throughout the years, they'd worked hard and paid their house off. Now the bedroom was silent, like the inside of a coffin, not to be morbid.

Someday he'd lie in one. Unless his family cremated him, which he preferred them not to do, but he understood it was less expensive. Even in death, money talked.

Whatever worked for them was fine with him. At that point in time, he wasn't going to care.

That was the way he felt about Trent's funeral too. Although, he tried to be involved, just because he knew Vera would want to see his interest and participation. It would say to her that he cared. Over the years, he'd learned that about her. When he didn't care, she saw it as a sign of disinterest, in her and in their relationship.

Maybe that was how she was feeling now.

He breathed out slowly, careful not to move and wake her. She was an extremely light sleeper. Whereas typically he lay down in bed and was asleep immediately, sleeping soundly, through pretty much anything.

Vera was the exact opposite. It took her forever to go to sleep, and when she did sleep, the slightest little thing would wake her up.

She seemed to sleep a little better when he was holding her, but that had stopped after the funeral.

She turned away and never turned back.

She was turned away right now, curled up in a little ball on the furthest part of her side of the bed.

He had to believe it was because she didn't want to have anything to do with him, and he didn't try to go over to her side and coax her out of her ball.

Maybe at first, he thought eventually she would turn back to him, but the months continued to slip by. He kept himself busy, deliberately so, and she had never rolled back over.

How could he have allowed their marriage to get to this point?

He blamed himself. He was the one who had taken on extra work. And he had done it without talking to Vera. Looking back, he assumed she knew that he needed to keep his mind occupied, to keep his hands busy, that he couldn't just sit around and think.

But it must have been a blow to her when he decided to landscape a personal residence in one of the Chicago suburbs.

It had been a ritzy house, a big job, and they had gotten plans made at the local landscaping warehouse. Dominic hadn't thought anything about it.

It wasn't like he was getting some other designer to make plans and working on a job with them. He just had the specs and did the job. It kept him busy.

Then he'd done another job with Vera, only it wasn't like before. It was like it was tonight. All business.

Then, she said that she had a couple of projects, but the designs weren't coming to her, and he got another suburban house to stay busy. And then, he had the opportunity to collaborate on a garden design for the city of Milwaukee.

That job had given him a little bit of pause, but Vera had been walking around the house in her nightgown, obviously not working. And he figured someone had to do something to pay the bills. So he'd taken the job.

Working with that design firm had not been like working with his wife, and while he did the same type of job that he always did, making sure everything was exact, nailing down the details, it...didn't feel as good.

He didn't think the design was as good either, and it certainly wasn't something that was going to win many accolades. That big design group definitely wasn't nearly as good as his wife.

But then, because of some work on a garden he and Vera had done in the city of Richmond, he'd gotten an offer to work with one of the nation's top designers, Shoshana Bolt.

That had been unexpected, and by then, he'd jumped on the chance. His reputation was growing, thanks to Vera, and this would be another feather in his cap. The pay probably wasn't as good as what he could have gotten, but he was so eager to work with Shoshana that he didn't care.

When he had agreed to work with her, she had promised him other jobs or at least hinted at a promise. He had looked at his schedule and figured that if Vera started designing again, he could hire another crew. He'd figure it out and make it all work, because building for Shoshana was maybe not a dream come true, but it was definitely a huge step on the way to his dream.

Of course, designing with Vera had been the start of the dream.

Sometimes he forgot that.

He had to admit, after that first residential job he'd done, he hadn't given Vera's feelings about him working with someone else another thought. It had already been done, and he figured she wouldn't care if it was done again. If it bothered her, she would have said something to begin with. But she didn't, so he continued.

And he'd been right about working with Shoshana. It had gotten him a lot of attention, and he couldn't keep up with all the work he was getting. All of it predesigned, but still, it was work. And paid extremely well.

That's when his income had surpassed hers.

He supposed, that's when the rift between them had widened. To what felt like an irrevocable place.

But nothing was irrevocable. He could fix this. He was a builder after all. That's what he did.

He rolled over, but it was a long time until he fell asleep, and even then, he slept fitfully, dreaming that Trent was still alive, but Vera had left him. And then he was a single dad, raising a son, and Shoshana was insisting he needed to do jobs for her, and she didn't understand that he had to spend time with his son.

He woke, not feeling rested at all but knowing even before he opened his eyes that the spot beside him on the bed was empty.

No matter how far away from him she slept, he could still feel her presence, and it was gone.

Not surprising, since Vera was an early riser. She most likely was out on the deck with a steaming cup of coffee, watching the sunrise.

Although, after looking at the clock, one bleary eye told him that the time was barely 4:30. Sunrise wouldn't be for another hour, and the sky probably wasn't even getting light yet.

But she'd be wrapped up in a blanket, her feet propped up on another chair, her eyes facing north or south. Probably south, so she could see both the eastern and western skies.

The sun rose in the east, of course, but it was beautiful when reflected off the water, which was west of their house.

He was tempted to go out and join her. They'd spent countless mornings watching the sunrise. When Trent was going through his toddler stage, that was the only time, other than the evenings and possibly a naptime, where they might have quiet time together. They cherished that time, just as much as they cherished the time with their child. After all, both of them wanted to nurture and care for their marriage.

He wasn't sure when that had stopped, but he was pretty sure it lay on his shoulders to do something about it.

After all, if the man was the head of house, it was the man's responsibility to make sure that things were going well at home, and that included the relationship he had with his wife, along with his children.

Of course, he didn't have to worry about that angle anymore.

He changed into jeans and a T-shirt, throwing a sweatshirt on because from experience the Michigan morning would be chilly until the sun rose and he could stand in its rays, getting warm.

Grabbing a cup of coffee, he went out to the back deck, which faced north, felt the crisp air, and decided what he would do for the day. For some reason, one of the main things on his list was avoiding his wife.

It would be hard to rebuild the relationship if he didn't make a point to see her, but he decided one more day to think about what he should do about her, and maybe they would have a talk tonight, over supper or before bed, and perhaps things would just magically work out.

Wishful thinking, but it came honestly, since he wasn't a relationship expert, didn't know much of anything about love, and had very little experience in lasting relationships.

The only relationship he had that lasted more than six months was his relationship with Vera. He probably should give her the credit she deserved for keeping them together. If it had been up to him, he probably would have allowed the relationship to fade off into the sunset, too busy with work and focused on building his business to notice there was a problem until it was so big it was almost insurmountable.

Like he'd done in the last year and a half.

With a shake of his head, he drank the last of his coffee and walked back inside. Maybe the healing garden would be healing in more ways than one.

Eight

Vera held her coffee in one hand, the blanket wrapped around her, and watched the sky slowly lighten. She had hoped that Dominic would come out and stand with her, her curled up in a blanket, he would have a sweatshirt on and pace or walk or otherwise burn energy and keep himself warm.

Of course, he'd have his coffee mug in hand as well.

But either he was sleeping in, or he wasn't coming out.

She supposed it didn't matter. Although there was definitely a sadness in her heart. Was it so very wrong for her to want to spend mornings watching the sunrise with her husband? Working somehow to get the relationship back on track? Or letting go completely.

She couldn't blame him. She was just as much to blame. But she didn't know how to fix it. Her coming out here, the way they often did, together, might be a first step, but either he was ignoring her first steps, or maybe there was someone else.

She shook that thought away. She thought that often through the last eighteen months. The way he wasn't interested in her, the way they didn't talk, the way he had a major project with her competitor—even though she and Shoshana were friends, although they had never met and they were definitely competitors as well, and to have her husband working for her competitor hurt her in a way that nothing ever had quite hurt her like that before.

It was a pain that irritated, constantly, whether she was thinking about it or not.

But she hadn't been designing anything, and she could hardly blame him for trying to find work, and it was definitely a boon for his business to have landed Shoshana as a designer.

If what she heard was true, he'd brought her designs to life just as beautifully as he did Vera's.

The sky had erupted in various shades of orange and red and pink and blues and greens, the lake reflecting it all back in beautiful brokenness, as the whitecaps swelled and broke.

It was windy out, and often that meant the sunrise wasn't as pretty, but it was a glorious one this morning, almost as though the Lord wanted to let her know that He saw her, and He wanted to do something special to make her smile.

Lord, if You want to do something special, You can make my husband interested in me again.

She didn't like praying that kind of prayer. She wanted to completely depend on God but do the work herself. Not that she didn't trust God to do it, she just didn't think that God blessed people who just sat around waiting for blessings to fall into their lap.

What was the saying? *Pray like it all depends on God, and work like it all depends on you.*

She should work, knowing that God could take the little bit she did and bless it in a huge way. She'd seen Him do that over and over in her life, and she figured He would do that now for her.

I don't know how to start, Lord.

She had sat outside, Dominic didn't come. She waited a little longer, and he still hadn't come. Now, she supposed she could go inside and see if...he wanted her to cook him breakfast?

She rebelled a little at the thought. She didn't want to serve him, not after what he'd done to her. Not after the way he'd neglected her, left her to wallow in her grief while he went and busied himself with his work. The idea that she would go in and humble herself enough to cook him a meal irritated her.

She shook her head. She didn't think that pride was something that she had a problem with. But maybe through this process, she was learning more about herself than was comfortable.

Determined that she would go in and offer to cook for her husband, make him a breakfast that he enjoyed, she straightened her legs out, took one last look at the fading colors of the sky and the way the lake shimmered them back, and then turned to walk in.

But the kitchen was empty when she walked in, and there wasn't a note on the counter.

Back, *before*, if he were going to leave, he would leave a note. But as she walked through the kitchen into the dining room and looked at the parking area outside the house, she could see his truck was gone.

Sitting on the other side of the house, she hadn't heard it and didn't realize.

Well, there went that idea. Part of her was relieved. A part of her felt justified. After all, she was coming in to do something nice for him, and he was leaving without even telling her where he was going or what he was doing. He was in the wrong, obviously.

Although, she suspected he was going down to measure the spot where they were planning to put the garden.

As she was thinking about it, she realized something that she hadn't thought about last night. In order to do a fountain, there was going to need to be a spot where they could hook into electricity.

The area where they were going to plant wasn't owned by anyone. The township had jurisdiction over it, and they'd already checked about that years ago when someone had suggested expanding the area for the tourists who came to visit the bluffs, although nothing ever came of it. As long as they didn't cost the township money, they were free to use it as they wished, but...somehow they were going to have to get electricity to the fountain, or it wasn't going to work. She couldn't believe that Dominic didn't say that last night. Maybe he already had an idea of what to do, but she wouldn't know.

Maybe this was the way he worked with Shoshana, although she doubted it.

She had to push that thought aside. She couldn't allow thoughts of Dominic and Shoshana working together to interfere with the work that she did with her husband. It was immature and childish, since after all, he was a professional. He was expected to work with other people.

Except, they had that unspoken agreement that they work only with each other.

That's what made their work so valuable, it was only available between the two of them.

It was like when they got married, the two of them became one, and that's what a person got when they got a Vera design. They got the best landscaper in the business. And if they wanted Dominic to do the landscaping, they needed Vera to do the design. That's just the way it was.

Deciding she wasn't going to sit around and ruminate over things she couldn't change, she spent a little bit of time in the sunroom, working on the designs but not really getting anywhere, and then when it was after ten, she decided that she'd go down and take a look at the ground herself. She was just getting up and gathering her things when the doorbell rang.

Dominic wouldn't be ringing the doorbell, of course, so she knew who it wasn't, although her heart still kicked up a few beats, like it hoped against hope that it was he.

Leaving things neatly arranged on the coffee table, she walked to the door and opened it.

"Gertie! It's been a while since I've seen you. Come on in," she said, opening the door wide for her neighbor and friend and giving her a smile and a hug as she walked in.

"You come and go so much now, I never know whether you're here or not. I saw Dominic down at the end of the road beside our house, and I walked out to chat with him, realized you were here, and figured I would pay a little call." She held up her empty hands. "If I had a little bit more warning, I would have made you something. My mom always said that a person shouldn't go visiting with empty hands."

"Well, I know your mom was a wise woman, but you're welcome here anytime, empty hands or no."

She really was happy to see her old friend, even if it did remind her a little bit of when Trent was alive, since Gertie had been a big part of the church before it closed.

"Would you like to sit in the sunroom? Or is it warm enough to sit outside?"

"Let's sit outside. It's a beautiful day, and after the winter we had, I'm always ready to spend as much time as possible in the sunshine."

"That's how I feel too," Vera said, although Dominic was the one who always got tanned and browned by the sun. Her work kept her inside, and it was a treat for her to be able to go out. "Would you like some iced tea? I'm sorry, I haven't been grocery shopping, and I don't have much in the way of food to offer you."

Gertie waved her hand. She must have been in her sixties, but she looked a decade younger. And her step had an energy in it that often faded as a person aged.

"I'm fine. I don't need to eat anything at all. I'll take some tea, if you're going to have some, but otherwise, don't bother. I didn't come to make more work for you. I just...miss you."

Vera, though at least twenty-five years younger than Gertie, considered Gertie a friend. And the idea that her absence, her retreat from community, had made Gertie sad made Vera feel that way as well.

"I'm sorry. I feel like maybe I'm just emerging from the fog I fell into after Trent's death." There she went, saying his name and only hesitating just a bit. "I haven't been a very good neighbor."

"No one expected you to be," Gertie said as she followed Vera to the sliding glass door, which Vera opened for her, and Gertie stepped out on the deck.

She took their teas to the table and set them down while Vera closed the door and set a bowl of grapes from the counter on the table as well.

"That's the best I can do," she said, waving her hand as though to offer Gertie whatever seat she wanted.

"Thank you. And that's better than I expected or wanted," Gertie said.

"So how are things going with you? Is Homer doing well?" Homer was Gertie's adult son, who did some kind of rocket science or computer programming or something along those lines, he was extremely intelligent and rather quiet.

But he participated in church and Sunday school and always had something a little bit deep, sometimes so deep Vera didn't quite understand it, to say. He had obviously studied his Bible and knew what he was talking about. Which was the kind of person Vera liked to be around, especially in church, but anywhere.

"Homer is doing great. His job is keeping him busy, and you know even though I told him that I would be fine living alone, he insists on staying with me. I don't think I'll ever get him married off."

Vera nodded her head, knowing that Gertie's husband had left her when Homer was eighteen. That had changed Homer's future plans. He had gone to community college, despite the fact that he had scholarships to more prestigious universities, so that he could stay home and be with his mother. He had finished his education in Ann Arbor and landed a well-paying job.

She wasn't sure, but she thought he might have continued his education at home some after he started working and perhaps had a master's degree or something at that point.

Regardless, the thing that she admired about Homer was the fact that he knew his mom would be alone if he left, and so he had given up the opportunity to possibly do more and had instead made sure that his mom was taken care of.

"Oh, I think the right girl will come along eventually. One who really appreciates him for who he is," Vera said, knowing that sometimes a future mate did not just fall in a person's lap, although that was what happened to her. She hadn't been particularly looking for someone when Dominic had come along. After one date, they both knew.

"What about you?" she added. "I'm sure you're staying busy. Although the church closing left a hole in Raspberry Ridge that I don't think anything else can fill." It was a small town, and the church had been the center of the community.

"I have some bad news myself, and I'm going to share with you, but only because I want you to know, not necessarily because I want you to do anything."

"Okay," Vera said cautiously, thinking that Gertie must have been diagnosed with cancer. Probably breast cancer. It was a common cancer, and so many women she knew had been stricken with it.

"My doctor said I have early-onset Alzheimer's. Actually, he recommended that I stop driving, but I feel like I'm in my right mind."

"You sound like it," Vera said, although her words came out in a bit of a shock. Early-onset Alzheimer's? That meant...she was losing a friend. She couldn't be sure, but she thought that she heard that early-onset Alzheimer's came on faster than the regular kind.

"Isn't there anything they can do?" Vera asked, hating the idea that Gertie might not be with her, even if she was still alive, much longer.

"I'm doing everything we can. There are some experimental medications, but I asked my son to be upright and honest with me, and Homer said he really didn't see a difference."

"Oh. That's terrible."

"Yeah. I'm not giving up, but...it's coming." She smiled and gave a little shrug, like there was nothing she could do, which was pretty much true.

Vera felt bad for her. She had had such bad luck with her husband leaving her, and she thought there was something else going on in years past. Gertie had always been a little evasive about it. But she considered Homer a miracle child, and then to find out that her husband had cheated, and she ended up being alone. Except for Homer. Who, Vera had to admit, was exactly the kind of man she hoped Trent would grow into.

Homer and Dominic were cut out of the same cloth. Honest and upright, with integrity and the kind of character that made them do the right thing, even when it was difficult. Even if they didn't want to. Of course, she didn't want Dominic to stay with her even though he didn't want to. She wanted him to want to.

Was that so terrible?

"Have you been to see Pastor and Mrs. Calvin?" Gertie took a sip of her tea like her news hadn't shocked Vera and made the sunny day suddenly seem gloomy and ominous.

"Not since they moved to their assisted living facility. I understand Mrs. Calvin is doing okay, but Pastor's eyesight is fading fast."

"The last time I went, he couldn't even see to read on the iPad his children had gotten him. It's...sad."

So much bad news. But she was coming out of her bad news, and she supposed her job was shifting to try to encourage others who were going through difficult times.

"Maybe I'll go see them."

"Dominic is here. Probably both of you should go together. He can visit with Pastor, while you visit with Mrs. Calvin. I think they'd love to see you both."

"Yeah. I'll...have to ask."

"I put the bug in Dominic's ear as well. Maybe he'll ask you." Gertie paused. "This is not my business, but the nice thing about Alzheimer's is I can confidently say that I probably won't remember anything you tell me."

She laughed a little, and Vera appreciated the fact that she had come to grips with her diagnosis and could even joke about it a little.

"But I noticed there seems to be a bit of a strain between you and Dominic. I thought after things settled down after Trent's funeral, things would go back to normal, but it doesn't seem like it has."

"They haven't." Vera spoke honestly. "And I don't know what to do about it."

She didn't typically confide in anyone over her marriage. She definitely would not speak badly of her husband to anyone, but here she was talking to Peggy and now to Gertie and admitting that she didn't know what to do.

"There just feels like there's this huge chasm between us, and I don't know how to cross it. I don't know what to do." She shrugged her shoulders.

"Because of Trent? Do you blame Dominic?"

"No. No, he reassured me that Trent wasn't as sick as he was, and maybe I would have taken Trent to the hospital sooner, but he said the best thing that he knew. It wasn't like he was trying to get me to not take Trent. For goodness' sake, he's allowed to make a mistake. That... That's sad, and it's hard to think about sometimes, but it's more hard because I wish I would have said, 'You know what, this doesn't feel right to me, I'm going to take him anyway.' And I know Dominic would have said, 'Okay. You do what feels right to you, I'll come home.'" She lifted her hands and slapped them down on the arms of her chair. "I know he would have. So no. I cannot possibly blame him for that."

"Then what's the problem? If I can ask."

Nine

"I'm talking. You might as well ask," Vera said with a little smile.

But she wasn't sure she could admit this: she was a little... jealous.

"Dominic and I worked together until Trent's funeral, and then I took a little bit of time off. It's perfectly normal, you know, I just... couldn't create very well. But he needed to keep busy, and so he took a garden job in some ritzy development in Chicago, which I understood, but then he was offered a very lucrative, very prestigious job building the design of a competitor of mine. She's also a friend, not a good friend, but someone I've spoken with online. Although we've never met, I would smile and make small talk with if I met her. But it hurt..."

There. She said it.

"Oh, honey. That *would* hurt. I understand." Gertie squeezed her hand, and Vera tried to make her smile real and not forced. But she needed to keep talking because she didn't want Gertie to think less of Dominic.

"I know there's nothing going on between them. At least, I think there's nothing going on between them. But everything else he did was a private job or something for a design company where they made the design and he implemented it. Not a big deal. But what he did with

Shoshana... I just... We didn't really ever say that we were going to be exclusive in our jobs, but I thought that we were. And maybe if he would have talked to me, maybe if he would have said, 'Hey, is this okay with you?'" Then she shook her head. "Actually, no. I would never have told him not to do it. His business has taken off faster and better than it ever would if he would have just stuck with me, and I would never have denied him that opportunity. It just hurts that he wanted it in the first place."

She tried to push the hurt aside. It felt more real, harder, when she talked about it. "People know him now because of her, and it was a good business decision on his part, but she has absolutely gotten business because of working with him and clients finding her because of her association with me. Basically he helped build my competitor's business by giving her access to everything I built. It...hurts."

She said it again. But that was the only way she knew how to describe it. What Dominic had done to her wasn't terrible, he hadn't double-crossed her, he hadn't cheated on her, he hadn't done anything awful, other than work for a competitor of hers. Or maybe just work for someone else, when up until that point, they'd been in unspoken agreement that they wouldn't. She wasn't sure exactly what the issue was, but every time she thought of it, it bothered her. And hurt.

"Do you want to stay married?" Gertie said, surprising Vera with her question.

She thought about it. She didn't want to give an off-the-cuff answer. She took her time when she spoke.

"I guess when I got married, I determined that divorce wasn't going to be an option. He didn't cheat on me, as far as I know."

"Even if he did, forgiveness is possible."

She wasn't sure whether she wanted to explore the idea of forgiveness if she was looking at cheating. That was a whole different story, but it did put things in perspective.

"I don't want to get divorced. I meant my vows when I said them, and I intend to stay married. I just... I feel like he's the one who walked away from me. I didn't go anywhere. He should be the one to make the first move to reconcile."

"Should he?" Gertie asked, a rhetorical question because she was nodding her head. "I agree. If he was the one who broke your unspoken agreement, walked off, then he should be the one to try to make amends, but are you gonna die on that hill?"

Vera hadn't thought about it like that.

"The Bible says that God resists the proud but gives grace to the humble. It takes humility to go to someone when you weren't the one who is wrong, and especially if they haven't even bothered to apologize. Maybe they don't even know they've done anything wrong, but if you're the one to go, you're the one to try to keep things together, that takes humility and God says He will give you grace."

Gertie looked down, as though she were gathering her thoughts, and then she said, "All through the Bible, God praises humility. He praises the one who's willing to give in. Think about Abraham and Lot. Their men were fighting. Abraham had seniority. He was in the right. He should have been the one to choose, but instead, he gave grace, showed humility, and allowed his nephew to choose. And we all know how that turned out."

God had blessed Abraham abundantly, and Lot ended up losing his wife, and his family was a mess after living with sodomites.

"Jesus showed true humility, more than any other human ever has, just from leaving heaven and coming down to earth and being born in a stable. It showed that God isn't interested in the biggest or the best or the loudest or the person who pushes their way the most. Sometimes we as humans have a tendency to label that strength. That's not strength, that's just being loud or pushy. Strength is actually being humble. That takes strength. And to go to your husband, when he doesn't deserve it, and be the first to reach out, and then continue to reach out if he doesn't respond, that's humility. If you want to save your marriage, that would be the path that I would choose, humility and forgiveness."

"Forgiveness is hard," Vera said flatly. It bothered her more than she realized that her husband had worked with her competitor. He had helped that woman achieve more than she would have achieved without him. He had helped her look good, had done his very best for her, maybe even better than he had done with Vera, since she was only his wife, but that was someone else, someone important, someone who was nationally recognized for their designs.

She had even looked on his website, and he had her design that he built featured. Of course he had Vera's on there too, but he had done a lot with Vera and only one with Shoshana, but Shoshana's design was front and center. More important than anything else. Like he was proud of it.

Maybe he was just proud of getting away from his wife, she didn't know. She couldn't let that stuff bother her. She had to...brush it aside.

"Forgiveness is hard, but you realize that forgiveness is just as much for you, maybe more so, than it is for the person who sinned against you. The person who sinned against you, your husband, he doesn't know, doesn't care, it doesn't matter to him. He's not suffering from it. You're the one that's caught in the bitterness and anger of what he did, of him walking away from you, neglecting you, not being there to support you after the loss of your son. And then, what he did with that other designer. Promoting her, breaking your agreement, and hurting your feelings."

Gertie looked like she was about to say something else, and Vera wondered if maybe she had some forgiveness that she'd been working on. Of course, her husband had left her for another woman, but Gertie didn't seem angry or upset about it.

"Sometimes the person that you have to forgive doesn't even ask for forgiveness. Sometimes you just have to let it go, let God handle it, because isn't that what we're doing when we refuse to forgive? We're saying, God can't handle this, so I have to. I have to make sure they suffer. I have to make sure that they're punished. I have to make sure that I'm angry and upset with them, and they know it, so they understand that they did something wrong, and they fall on their knees and apologize to me."

Gertie raised her brows. "I don't know about you, but I thought those things. I'll punish him until he realizes what he did, and then he can grovel and I'll think about forgiving him. That's not what God wants at all."

No. It wasn't what God wanted, and it was clear to her now, although it hadn't been clear before.

But still.

"It's hard. I know you're right, but I just don't want to. I want him to see what he did wrong, I want him to feel bad. I want him to have regrets. I want him to realize that whatever he did with Shoshana ruined what he had with me. It made us…less, because instead of having something exclusive, he opened himself up to anyone. And I guess it made me feel insecure too, because Shoshana is such a great designer, nationally recognized, far more than me, and it kind of felt like he didn't want me, he wanted her."

Gertie nodded, her eyes holding compassion and sorrow, but also wisdom.

"I know how we feel often dictates how we act, but if we can divorce ourselves from how we feel and act in a way that's right and not based on how we feel, we'll be so much further ahead. You do admit in your head, maybe not in your heart, but in your head, you need to forgive your husband and let the past go, whether he requests forgiveness or not. Just because that's good for your health."

"I admit that. Yes."

"Then you just have to get over your feelings. Right?"

"Yeah. But that's a lot harder to do than it sounds like. Because I can feel myself resisting every time I think, I'll just let it go, I'll just let it go and I'll let God handle it. I don't want to be in the revenge business. I don't want to make people feel bad, especially not my husband because I love him. I don't want to rub his face in what he's done wrong and make sure he understands that he is supposed to honor and respect me, and he didn't. God can make sure of that. I believe that. I just…want to help, you know. Kind of push things along a little bit."

"I know exactly what you mean. But looking back on my life, which is a little bit longer than yours, every single time that I tried to push things along, make them work out the way I wanted them to, help God out, if you will, I ended up worse off than I was to begin with."

"Thank you. I hope I can learn from your mistakes, not continuously have to make the same mistake over and over again until I figure things out. I think I've held onto my grudge long enough. I mean, originally we really did grow apart because of Trent's death, and we each had different ways of coping. But his way of coping hurt my feelings, and it just went downhill from there, I guess."

"Well, it's good that you know exactly what happened, because sometimes we need to know that in order to set in motion the things that have to happen in order for everything to get better."

They chatted for a bit more, the conversation taking a turn to other things, and Vera thought about how much she was going to miss her friend.

Before Gertie left, Vera said, "I don't want to be morbid, and I don't want to remind you about this if you didn't want to talk about it, but... once your Alzheimer's," she stumbled over the word, "has taken over, do you have any requests?"

"I told my son the only thing I wanted was to stay at home. I wonder sometimes if maybe that request is a little selfish. After all, I've seen memory care patients, and sometimes they need to be in a locked room because they're an escape hazard. They'll hurt themselves, but... I would rather walk out my door and drown in the lake than be taken from my home and locked in a little room in a care facility somewhere. What's the point of a life like that?"

That was a good question. She wasn't sure what the point of life was if you had to be locked away in a room. You weren't teaching anyone character by making them have to take care of you, and you weren't enjoying it yourself.

"Sometimes I wonder why God allows us to suffer so much when we get older. And I finally came to the conclusion that partially it was for our character building, but partially it was for others' character. You know? Like it takes character to take care of someone who doesn't know who they are, or where they're at, or..." She wanted to say where the bathroom was, but she didn't want to be too graphic and make Gertie get depressed. Although Gertie seemed to have a better handle on life than she did and seemed more content, even though she knew that her moments of enjoying it were limited.

"That's a good point. I've wondered myself why God would allow this to happen to me. Why not just to me, to everyone. Why do we suffer, but in particular, why would I suffer, not even knowing who I am, what I'm doing, what's the point in that? I can't really build character when I don't even know my name. Or don't even know the people around me. You might be right. Maybe God's going to use me to grow someone else. It's...humbling for sure."

"I bet it is."

And maybe that's what God had done with Dominic. He was using Dominic and his, she assumed, innocent decision to team up with Vera's rival to grow Vera and make her a better person.

"God must have seen some rough edges in me that need to be shaved off. And I've been very resistant to allowing Him to shave them."

Vera could see that now. She hadn't wanted to grow; she wanted her husband to be the one to grow. The one to see his mistakes and come groveling to apologize.

But that wasn't God's plan. God's plan was for her to overlook Dominic's inconsideration, especially in light of the death of their son, and love him anyway.

Just love him anyway.

She thought about that long after Gertie had left. That was the point. That was the hard things that they had talked about in their marriage vows. The times when things weren't going to be perfect, when people were going to do things that upset them, when stumbling blocks happened, like the death of one's son, and when one was sensitive and in a delicate mental state, offenses came, and Vera's job was to *love her husband anyway.*

Thankful that the scenario that Gertie had suggested, her husband cheating on her, was not what she was dealing with, she wondered if she would be able to forgive in that situation.

Could she love him anyway like she had vowed in her marriage vows?

She was allowed to divorce in that scenario, and she was pretty sure that if she were dealing with cheating, she would almost certainly seek divorce, because she didn't want to live with a man who couldn't keep his promise. But she couldn't say for sure, until she was in that position.

Whatever Dominic had done, she was pretty sure it didn't involve cheating.

Lord, help me to overlook his faults, forgive the offenses that I've seen that he might not even know about, and help me to love my husband anyway.

Ten

Dominic set his saw down on the two-by-four and picked up the end that he had just cut off. This was the last piece he needed to cut and screw in, and then the planter that he made for around the other side of their house would be finished.

He'd have put it together out in the yard, but since a cold front had moved in, bringing rain with it, he'd been working in the garage since he'd gotten home from measuring the plot of land, looking it over, renting the bulldozer, and talking to Homer.

He'd also walked down the trail by the bluffs to the pebble beach at the bottom.

It was true that their son Trent loved the sandy beach at Blueberry Beach much better than he liked the pebbles at the bluffs, but it might have been because the sand was novel and exciting, and he didn't get to go there very often.

Whatever it was, Dominic preferred the pebble beach. The soft stones had been worn smooth by the motion of Lake Michigan's waves over the centuries, and Dominic enjoyed taking his shoes off and walking on the beach.

He spent a lot of time thinking, and when he got home, he walked around the downstairs of the house, looking for his wife. He found her in the sunroom, working.

Not wanting to interrupt her, he went out to the garage and spent the rest of the afternoon doing something that would keep his mind off all the things that were swirling in his brain, because he was happiest when his hands were busy. When he was thinking about building something, creating something and putting it together. Following specs and making something that was just pieces of stuff into something beautiful.

Of course, Vera had made the specs for their yard years ago, and he'd been slowly working at bringing her designs to life. Neither one of them had been in a huge hurry to get it all done; they enjoyed the journey just as much as they enjoyed the final destination when it came to enjoying designs.

Especially their own.

But maybe he waited a little too long, since it was almost eight o'clock when he put his tools away and closed the garage door, walking into the house. If Vera had eaten, he couldn't tell. Of course, she cleaned up everything behind her religiously, although he had suggested after their son was born maybe she needed to loosen up a little, and she tried. He had to hand it to her, she had tried.

But since his death, she'd gone right back to the way she had been. It was hard for him to fault her in that. He knew that she drew peace and security out of order and keeping things neat. Just the way he drew peace and security from working with his hands and creating things.

In a similar way he needed to keep busy after Trent's death, Vera had withdrawn, retreating into herself, to think about it and ponder.

Their differences were part of what made them so compatible. He was outgoing and friendly, she was a little more reserved, he worked with his hands, she worked with her mind. Not that his job didn't require intelligence, and not that she didn't get her hands dirty at times, but their gifts weren't in those areas. They complemented each other, and he'd always loved how nicely they seemed to go together.

He still hadn't figured out what he was going to do to try to win her back. Because that seemed to be what needed to be done. Win her back. But where did he start? She seemed so cool and unaffected by him. And maybe him going off and working with other people had upset her. He worried about that some last night and couldn't sleep.

It looked like he might be thinking about the same things tonight, since she wasn't in the sunroom, and the kitchen looked just as pristine as it had when he left this morning.

He was trying to think of what he could say when he walked into the kitchen, leaning against the counter, eating a sandwich that he put together for himself, when his phone buzzed.

Maybe one of the jobs that he'd been waiting to hear he got approval for had come through.

He just about choked on the sandwich when he saw the text was from his wife.

Would you like to go with me to visit Pastor and Mrs. Calvin tomorrow? I was thinking about leaving around 10.

He stared at his phone. Reading the text over and then over again.

He closed his eyes, his phone dropping to his side.

How long had it been since she had invited him to do something with her?

He knew exactly how long, and he could hardly believe it.

Pulling his phone up, he read it again. Yes. She was inviting him to go. There were no heart emojis, or smiley faces, or silly side jokes, as she might have done at one time, but it was a start. She was reaching out to him. Although, he'd always had a great relationship with Pastor Calvin, and she probably knew that he really would want to go see him. But she hadn't had to invite him to go. She could have just gone herself.

Then he realized he'd been sitting there, not answering her text. Maybe she thought that he didn't want to go and was trying to talk himself into it or something.

Pulling his phone up, he stared at her text again, reading it one more time, trying to formulate an answer in his head. One that didn't sound too eager, because he didn't want to come across like he was a teenage kid who had just had the most popular girl in the school ask him out, although that's kind of how he felt. But he also didn't want to come across as cool and uninterested, and only doing it to appease her, not because he wanted to.

I've been wanting to go see him for a while. Thanks for inviting me. I'll be ready to go at 10.

The fact that they were texting each other, while she was in one part of the house and he was in the other, and they could easily, within a few minutes, if not seconds, find each other and talk face-to-face, was not lost on him.

But the fact that they were even talking at all was nothing short of a miracle.

He realized that he was holding his sandwich, forgotten, in his other hand.

Keeping a hold of his phone in case she texted him back, he took another bite and chewed thoughtfully.

He had been praying that God would help him figure out a way to get to his wife, to bridge the rift that seemed to be between them, and it made him feel a little bit less of a man that Vera had taken the first step. He should have been the one to take the lead.

He remembered the Bible story about Deborah, when there were no men who were willing to lead the army of Israel. They were all too scared, too afraid they were going to lose the fight and die, so Deborah had done it.

But it was a shame for Israel, that a woman had had to take the reins and do what the men wouldn't do.

He knew that story, and yet, he was in his marriage, allowing his wife to take the lead and do the hard thing.

He hung his head.

Lord, Vera is the Deborah in our marriage, and yet, she'd always been so willing to allow me to lead. Willing to be submissive to me and make me the head of our home. And it's fine, when everything's going well, and I'm making the easy decisions. But we had something hard, have something hard. It's been happening for a long time, and she took the lead, while I stood back. I'm sorry. That's not a good look, and I'd really like to be better. Please help me, help me figure out how to take the lead in repairing our relationship.

Eleven

Vera had slipped from bed before her husband again the next morning. She watched the sun come up where she normally did, and to her surprise, as the sky lightened, he came out on the porch.

She stayed wrapped in her blanket, holding her coffee, and he held his, walking the way he usually did, occasionally stopping to look, and then walking around some more. He seemed to think better when his body was moving. While she thought better when she was completely still.

It was a difference that had always fascinated her.

Nonetheless, they didn't say a whole lot. Typically, Dominic wasn't very chatty in the morning. It was the one time of day where he was more likely to grunt than anything.

Her heart had squeezed with hope, and she wanted to smile as she lifted her face to the lake breeze and watched the orange light dance on the water.

It was chilly, and she went back in. His phone rang as she had started to get up, so they never said anything.

Although, as she was sliding the door closed, she heard him say, "Hey, Shoshana, what's up?"

Her heart stiffened in her chest.

It was an odd time of day for a business call.

She tried not to let that ruin her mood. But she hurried through the kitchen, taking her coffee cup with her and going straight to the sunroom where she turned some heat on before she sat down and opened her laptop.

If she was working, Dominic wouldn't bother her. He wouldn't interrupt her unless it was an emergency.

And she didn't want to talk to him right then.

Obviously, he and Shoshana were still talking, even if they weren't working together, but she didn't know. Maybe they had another project planned. It wasn't like he was sharing his schedule with her. It used to be that they went over their schedules together. Of course...she had access to his schedule. She just hadn't looked at it.

That was on her. He hadn't removed her. Her eyes widened. At least she didn't think he had.

So, rather than working, she opened her laptop and went immediately to the website where they shared their schedules and kept all their business information.

It was a handy little thing where they could keep all of their notes, and she could even upload her designs, although she never had. He could keep his list of materials and keep track of the hours that he worked on each project as well.

He used it a lot more than she did, which was why she was never on it. She only did one design project at a time, and typically she wasn't so overbooked that she needed some kind of help to keep track of everything.

Pulling up his calendar, she felt a little...like she was doing something wrong. But she wasn't. They often looked at each others' schedules. Back when they talked and worked together, she knew exactly what he was doing and when he was doing it, and if she didn't, or if she needed an update or a refresher, she just pulled up the schedule and checked. It wasn't a big deal. Except, now she felt like she was spying on him. And she supposed that was because of her attitude and reasons for going in there in the first place. But it was a little bit odd that Shoshana would be calling him so early.

Regardless, she brought the schedule up and saw that he had four jobs that were pending approval. Wow. He was really busy. He had another one scheduled and was bidding on six more.

That seemed like a lot, but she didn't know a whole lot about the bidding process. The little bit that she had bid on projects, she had learned that a person didn't get every project they bid on. In fact, they might not get any of the projects they bid on.

Since he was so busy, he might have bid high on those projects, which would make them worth his time.

Regardless, Shoshana wasn't on the schedule.

Relieved, she clicked out of the application and opened her design app. She didn't know why she was having so much trouble with these last two areas, but nothing seemed to be right. She just couldn't quite get the exact tone and feel that she wanted.

Deciding that maybe she needed to browse different plants, she pulled up a site and lost herself in her work. Which was exactly what she needed.

Her husband was not cheating on her, they had just grown apart. It felt like a chasm between them, but it wasn't unbridgeable, and they would get through this. She had made the first step in reaching out, and they were going to be spending time together later that day. In the meantime, she would focus on her work, finish designing the garden, and then maybe she'd look through offers that she had in the recent past and see if any of them were still open. She felt like maybe she'd be ready to work again, and soon.

Of course, she didn't know for sure that her husband would be available to do the landscaping for her design.

But if he wasn't, she'd do what every other designer did and either hire her own landscaper or inform the applicant when she sent her acceptance that she would only be providing the design for this project.

She did not need to elaborate.

Organizing everything in her mind made her feel a lot better, and she was able to lose herself in her work, long enough so that when she finally came up for air and glanced at her watch, it was just a few minutes until ten and almost time to leave.

She was never late. Usually she set an alarm on her phone if she knew she was going to be immersing herself in her work and might lose track of time.

Saving her work and closing her computer quickly, she organized everything neatly and decided that she might have time to run upstairs and fix her hair. Maybe even change her clothes.

She was still in the outfit that she put on this morning, which was fine for visiting, but...she was actually going to be with her husband for the first time in a year and a half, maybe she should wear something that was a little bit more flattering to her figure and her coloring.

She'd just thrown this on in the dark.

As she hurried out of the sunroom, she glanced out the window at the area where their vehicles were parked, and she saw her husband, phone to his ear, standing in front of his pickup talking.

Interesting that he had been on the phone when she went into her office, and he was still on when she came out. Of course, his work involved a good bit of talking on the phone, but the last call she knew about had been Shoshana. He wasn't still talking to her, was he?

She put her hand over her stomach and resisted the urge to double down. She couldn't believe how much that hurt. The idea of him not just working with Shoshana but talking on the phone with her too. Chatting. Of course, Vera knew from experience that if he was going to partner with someone, it meant talking to them. Meant discussing things. It wasn't a one and done.

In some cases, it could be. The designs could all be laid out, and the builder could just build, but the best relationships, the ones that went to the next level, were a dynamic relationship, where there was give-and-take, where the designer and the builder worked together.

Maybe it wasn't totally commonplace, but she thought it was catching on more in the industry, particularly because she and Dominic had led the way.

She sucked in a breath and decided that she wasn't going to change her clothes after all. The jeans and fitted shirt she put on this morning would be just fine.

She grabbed a sweater, threw it over her shoulders, and slipped her feet into the ballet flats that sat by the door.

Part of her wanted to make herself look her very best for her husband. After all, if Shoshana was going after her husband, Vera could guarantee that Shoshana was looking her very best while doing it. But it shouldn't be about looks. It shouldn't be about what he saw when he looked at her, it should be about what was underneath all of that. After all, a person couldn't help the looks that they were born with.

Maybe Shoshana was beautiful on the inside as well. Maybe she was a loving, caring, compassionate person who deserved Dominic's admiration and attention, but that didn't change the fact that Dominic was married. He was *her* husband.

Of course, she hadn't been a very good wife lately.

She swallowed past that thought. Not liking it, but recognizing the truth in it.

Well, she was going to try to change that. She was going to try to be a better wife, and she was not going to allow her subconscious to mess with her head about Dominic and Shoshana. As far as she knew, her husband was an honorable, upright, honest man. He would never cheat on his wife.

Until she had absolute evidence to the contrary, she was not going to believe the rumors in her head. Instead, she was going to work on being a better wife and trying to fix the mess she made of her marriage. After all, she did want to stay married.

She loved Dominic, but even if she didn't, even if the feelings weren't there, she had made vows, and she was a woman of her word. She would keep them.

Taking a breath, saying a silent, quick prayer that she could put into practice the things she was thinking and not go back to her old habits, the ones she fell into after her son died, she twisted the knob and stepped outside.

Twelve

Dominic pressed off on his phone and watched his wife come down the stairs.

He just turned down one of the jobs that he'd bid on. And after that, he sent off two emails, pulling his bids from four of the six that were pending. They were hard emails to write, but he realized last night that he hadn't been paying attention to his marriage the way he should have been, and he'd woken up this morning with a fresh, urgent urge to do something about it.

He had worked to keep busy, and it had been effective for him, but then he'd gotten addicted to it. Addicted to the success, to the accolades, to all of the glory and honor that came with doing a great job and being wanted and in demand.

Sure, he wanted his business to be successful. He got some of his identity from being a good landscaper, but he'd lost some of his identity too, because his wife wasn't beside him. She was back...with Trent somewhere.

"You look beautiful this morning," he said, and he realized that the words were out of his mouth before he thought about them, although they were good words. He should give his wife compliments, because she was beautiful. To him. Since beauty was subjective. Not everyone agreed on what beauty was, but it didn't matter to him. Whatever the rest of the world wanted to think about the rest of the women in the world, he didn't care. His wife was beautiful.

She paused as she took a step down, her eyes flying to his, surprise lifting her face.

Yeah. His wife shouldn't be surprised when he gave her a compliment. That definitely said it had been way too long. She should expect compliments, be beaming when he said them, maybe, but not be totally shocked that he even managed to get something nice out of his mouth.

"Why are you looking so surprised? Don't you think you're beautiful?"

"Maybe once upon a time. Back when we were dating, were first married, but that was a decade ago, and I was a lot younger."

"Young does not mean beauty to me. *You* equal beauty."

He had to push that out, because normally he had his mind preoccupied with all the things he had to do. Even when they worked together, he thought about the job, the things he did, what was happening the next day, what he needed to schedule in the next week. He didn't think about his wife as a person necessarily, and he wasn't sure when he had lost that.

"That's very kind of you to say," she said, and it sounded a little formal. Vera always was a little classy. Not standoffish, exactly, just...not the kind of girl that skipped around going, *hey, thanks, dude.*

"Thank you," she ended, continuing to walk down the stairs.

He watched her for a little bit, noticing the changes in her.

She was right, she was older. There were more lines around her eyes, more around her mouth, because she did smile a lot. Maybe she wasn't quite as slim as she used to be. In fact, now that he looked, she definitely wasn't as slim as she used to be. And instead of trailing her fingers on the banister as though in contemplation, she held onto it like she needed it for her balance.

She still wore the ballet flats, and maybe her ankles weren't as trim as they used to be as they peeked out of her skinny jeans, but it was his wife. Of course he loved her and thought she was beautiful.

But she could hardly know that if he didn't tell her, and he remembered having a conversation back in the early days of their marriage where she had asked if he loved her, and he had told her, "I told you I loved you. Why are you asking?" And she explained that just because he said it once didn't mean that she didn't think that maybe he had changed his mind.

She was almost to his truck, and he realized he could run around and open her door. He felt a little bit like an idiot as he took three quick steps to catch up to her and then put a hand on her waist as he reached around to open the door.

The shock in her eyes as her head swiveled to stare at him would have been ludicrous, except...when did he quit opening her door?

Sometime after Trent was born? No. Sometime after Trent had died. He had always been aware that he needed to show his son how a man treated a woman. He needed to model that behavior so his son knew exactly what he should do. Not that Dominic felt like he had all the answers, but he had learned a few things in his marriage, and he wanted his son to grow up just knowing those things.

But then, when Trent died, he supposed things had fallen by the wayside when he had gotten busy.

"Thank you," she murmured after she had paused for at least three seconds, looking at him as though trying to figure out what in the world he was doing.

"Sorry I haven't done that for a while."

She had gotten in and adjusted herself in the seat, reaching back to put her seat belt on.

"It's been a while since we've ridden anywhere together." There was no censure in her words, and he didn't think they were said to make him feel guilty, but they did. She was right. They hadn't ridden together anywhere for a while.

He closed her door thoughtfully, thinking about the schedule ahead and what he had just seen on it earlier that day.

He walked around the front of the pickup and got in. He had started it and was putting his belt on when he looked over at her and said, "You're right. We haven't gone anywhere for a while. We still have those tickets to go to the ten-year anniversary of the first garden we made. It's by the Monongahela River in Pittsburgh. Remember?"

"I remember, that was probably one of my favorites. There was so much to work with, with the reflection of the river and the motion of the water, and the skyline of Pittsburgh in the background."

Yeah. They'd worked on that, and both of them had been excited. It had been their first job together, the first big job, ever, for either of them, and he and Vera had stayed up late night after night after night, talking and dreaming and knowing that if they could nail this, they could be not just a couple in marriage, but a couple of towering reputation in their respective businesses, and creating a niche all their own, with the two of them working together.

Great duos down through history had gone through their imagination. Rodgers and Hammerstein had been suggested by Vera, since she was more into music, at least that type, than he was.

Paul and Silas. Bonnie and Clyde. That one had made them laugh. They'd been young and so optimistic.

He pulled out onto the road. "Are we still going to the tenth anniversary celebration?"

"Do you want to?" she asked, looking over and lifting her brows as though she wasn't sure.

She'd been out of the loop for a long time, and maybe she hadn't remembered that they'd committed to going.

"Yes. We have the airline tickets. They booked us a place to stay, and they're hoping we'll both say a few words. I didn't give a commitment to that, but I know they wanted it."

"I haven't seen anything about that in my inbox."

"We gave them the email to our shared calendar. That's where all the messages are."

"Oh."

Maybe it was his imagination, but she looked a little guilty.

"It's a little late to cancel, but I can give them your regrets if you don't want to go. I really want you to. It's...been a while since we've done much together, and I miss you."

There seemed to be some kind of vulnerability in her gaze when she looked over across the seat at him, like he was being too nice to her, which was sad. All he'd done was give her a few compliments this morning and then told her he missed her, after he hadn't done anything with her for a year and a half.

He should have missed her after a day. It shouldn't have taken him a year and a half to wake up and realize that he hadn't been a very good husband.

But by God's grace, he was going to continue to try to put one foot in front of the next, adjusting his course so that he handled things correctly from now on.

"Do you?" she asked finally, looking at her hands in her lap before looking out the window as the houses of Raspberry Ridge disappeared behind them.

"Yes. I do. I miss you a lot."

"That's nice," she said, and he was a little taken aback. What did that mean? *That's nice?*

It's nice that he missed her? Shouldn't she say something about missing him too? Or being glad that he missed her and then say that they should do more things together?

He wasn't quite sure what to make of that. And for the first time, something like panic seemed to form in a ball in his stomach. What if he'd waited too long? What if it was too late for him to change direction and start walking in a different way? What if he'd already lost her?

No. Surely not. Vera was as straightlaced and honest as a person came. She would not walk away from him, just because they'd gone through a hard time and he buried himself in work. She would honor her vows no matter what. He knew that about her.

Except, he got the feeling that maybe he didn't know her as well as he thought. A year and a half was a long time, and a person could make a lot of changes in that time period.

She'd been right beside him, somewhere, all that time, but he hadn't paid attention.

"I'd forgotten about it, but if you want me to go, I can."

"I want you," he said without hesitation.

He wanted to say more, wanted to ask what happened to them. He always felt like they had such a solid, strong relationship.

Of course, Vera would have loved to have more children, but she couldn't. Or it might have been him, they'd never gotten tested. He would never have minded that either, but he had been perfectly and completely content with his life with Trent and Vera.

He loved that life. Why had he taken it for granted? Why had he taken her for granted?

He wanted to ask if it was too late, but they were coming up on the outskirts of Blueberry Beach, and he needed to pay attention to get the right turn to get to the nursing facility.

Everything was new, and just in time for Pastor Calvin and his wife, since they'd moved not long after the nursing home had been opened. Pastor Calvin had needed it since his eyesight had been getting so bad, and Mrs. Calvin hadn't been strong enough to take care of him or pick him up if he fell, which, from what Dominic understood, he did a good bit.

They were silent as he maneuvered through the roads, finally reaching the nursing facility. He didn't remember what room number Pastor and Mrs. Calvin were in, but he knew which section of the building they needed to enter from the last time he visited.

Had it really been over a year ago?

It'd been cold, snowing, and they had just moved into the room. The church had been closed since Christmas, which was when they had shuttered the doors, making the Christmas Day service the last service the church housed.

Unless someone else opened it.

Which Dominic desperately wished someone would, because he needed it.

"I don't remember the room number," he announced as he pulled into the visitor parking section.

"Four twenty-six," Vera said easily.

She didn't have a photographic memory, but she did have a good head for design, and he would be willing to bet that she could tell him exactly what the plaque on Pastor and Mrs. Calvin's door looked like, which was probably where she got the number from, that image she had stored in her head.

He didn't know how she did it, but he'd always admired that about her. Her brain was so much different than his. Intelligent, just in a different way.

She complemented him so beautifully. Surely he wasn't going to lose that.

"Of course. I knew you would remember," he said, snapping off his seat belt and grabbing his wallet from the console.

From what he recalled, the facility had a little snack shop, where they could grab some ice cream or something after they visited. It wouldn't exactly be a date, but maybe he could get his wife to go in with him.

Just...break the ice somehow. Because, yeah, that's how it felt, there was ice around their relationship, and he felt like he was stiff and couldn't move.

She had gotten herself out by the time he got out, and they walked to the door side by side before he opened it for her.

He opened the second door as well, smiling a little when she paused in front of it waiting.

He had been with women who insisted on opening their own doors, and while he knew that Vera was very capable of doing it herself, he appreciated that she allowed him the privilege.

It made him feel...manly.

Vera had always made him feel manly. She was just as capable, just as smart, just as successful, and in fact in the early days of their relationship up until the last year, she had been more successful than him.

But she never made him feel less than because she was every bit as good as he, and she never made it into a competition, where she was proving every second that she could be just as good as a man. In fact, without even realizing she did it, she stepped back and allowed him to go forward, to make decisions, decisions she was perfectly capable of making but she gave him deference, submitted to him, and lived the biblical role that God had laid out for a woman with such effortless ease that he hardly ever noticed.

He missed that when he designed with someone else, because they weren't Vera. They didn't have her class and her ability to make him feel like a man while not diminishing herself in any way.

They smiled at the lady at the front desk, but neither one of them said anything other than good morning as they made the left turn and walked down the hallway.

He put his hand on the small of her back as they turned, less about guiding her and more about...touching her. That's what he did when she was beside him, he touched her. She used to touch him all the time. But it had been a year and a half since she had walked by him and touched him for no reason.

He missed that.

She did not try to shake off his hand, which he appreciated. And he dropped it as they got to the set of elevators.

He had no idea why the rooms on the second floor started with four, but that was the floor they were going to, and he pushed the button after they got in.

They were the only ones in the elevator as the doors closed with a soft thump in front of them.

It was quiet as the machine rolled up, slowing before coming to a stop as the light lit on the number two and the bell dinged.

He didn't used to have these long, uncomfortable silences with her.

It wasn't that they talked all the time, but usually they would be having a small conversation, maybe about the pastor and his wife, the things they appreciated about them, their concerns, even the church.

Did they really have nothing to talk about now?

The doors opened, and he put his hand on the small of his wife's back again as she stepped forward, leading him out.

There was a big open area, where several older folks in wheelchairs sat, some of them taking a midmorning nap, some of them staring out the window, all of them looking a little sad. Despite the sunny day outside and the promise of spring, the flowers blooming and the air warming.

They couldn't know it, with the temperature-controlled air inside. Summer and winter must have felt pretty much the same.

Scanning his eyes over the room, Dominic said, "I don't see Pastor or Mrs. Calvin."

"I don't either," Vera said, making another left-hand turn and heading toward the hallway where the room was.

He put his hand on the small of her back yet again as she turned, feeling her warmth under his fingers, the movement of her body, graceful and sure. Although not quite as sure as it used to be. He could feel a little bit of wobbling there and realized that she was right. They really were getting older.

Maybe that was another reason he kept so busy, so he could keep inconvenient truths like that at bay.

They reached the door, and Vera stopped in front of it, squaring her shoulders and facing it.

It was almost as though she were gathering her nerve. But he knew she wasn't shy or retiring, and she enjoyed chatting with people, so he wasn't quite sure what that was all about.

Standing beside her, he raised his hand and knocked.

Thirteen

Vera didn't understand what had gotten into her husband.

Was God answering her prayers that quickly?

Why did she pray and then act all surprised when God answered?

Except, it felt odd, after all of the time that had passed where they had barely spoken to each other, where he hadn't seemed to notice her at all, and then all of a sudden, he tells her she's beautiful, opens her door for her, and now he's putting his hand on the small of her back and gently offering support as she walks.

That was just odd.

She tried to shake the feeling away, tried to pretend that there wasn't anything weird going on, but at the same time, she was on guard.

Was he going to let her know that he wanted a divorce now? Was that what this was leading to? Did he want her to not throw a fit and try to get more than her "share" in the divorce settlement?

Maybe he wanted to take more than his share.

No. That wasn't Dominic. There might be some distance between them, and they might have grown apart in the last year and a half, but Dominic was not a jerk. He might have made some bad decisions, he might possibly have had a relationship with Shoshana that she didn't want to know about, but Dominic wasn't a jerk.

That was one thing she was sure of.

"Come on in, the door's open," someone called through the door as they waited.

Dominic opened the door, put his hand over her head, and pushed it open so she could walk in first.

He'd always been considerate like that. That was nothing new. Opening doors, allowing her to go on and off the elevator first, that was normal.

She smiled a little, because he had wanted to be a good example to his son, so his son grew up knowing how a man was supposed to treat his woman.

Dominic should have had twenty children, so he could model that, so he could raise sons to grow up in the world who were courteous and well mannered.

"Pastor!" Vera said as she came around the recliner and stood in front of Pastor Calvin. His old eyes, rheumy yet still vivid blue, widened at the sound of her voice.

"That's Vera Miller," he said.

"It sure is, and Mrs. Calvin, it's so nice to see you," Vera said, giving Mrs. Calvin a hug as Dominic must have grabbed Pastor's hand and placed it in his, because when she moved back from the hug, they were shaking.

"I wasn't expecting visitors today," Mrs. Calvin said.

"Well, it's been a while, and I feel bad about that," Vera said as Mrs. Calvin moved a few things from the loveseat that made up the other piece of furniture in the room, beyond the two recliners, to make room for her guests to sit down.

"Do you want to have a seat? I hope you came to chat."

"We sure did."

There was a TV in the corner, but it was off, dark and silent, and the end table between the two recliners was filled with books and papers and a couple of pencils and a box of tissues. The light was small, with a short chain hanging down, but modern enough to have plugs in which a person could charge their phones or iPads.

"We were just listening to a book on tape."

Vera smiled, imagining that Pastor and Mrs. Calvin were actually listening to an audiobook, but she was using the old-fashioned terminology.

"That's a nice way to spend a morning," Dominic said.

"Actually, I'd kind of like to take a walk. I have to be careful where I go, because Edna May gets worried that I might fall down. But with a big, strapping fella like this beside me, I could probably get permission to go. Do you mind, Dominic?"

"Not at all, Pastor. I'd love to take a walk with you. It's nice outside, if you want to go there."

"I'd love to lift my face to the lake breeze. I miss it."

Mrs. Calvin smiled indulgently as her husband felt around for his cane. She put it in his hand, and he lifted himself from the chair.

"Hope you don't mind if I grab a hold of you, son," Pastor said as he took hold of Dominic's arm.

Vera wasn't sure whether she was relieved or disappointed that she didn't have to sit in the loveseat with her husband.

She supposed she was relieved—if he had been talking to Shoshana that day. But beyond that, she was disappointed. Deeply so.

They didn't say much until the men had left the room, and then Mrs. Calvin sat down in her recliner.

"I'm so sorry I can't offer you any refreshments. It feels like I should. But we just have a mini fridge, which is not enough to put a whole gallon of tea in. I just have a quart in there, for Pastor and myself, although you're welcome to some if you'd like."

"No thank you. I didn't come for you to serve me. I wanted to visit a bit. It's been so long."

"You've been in my prayers."

She got right to the heart of the matter, didn't she? Of course, it had been a year and a half. Mrs. Calvin probably expected that Vera had gotten over things by now.

"I feel like the fog is finally lifting, but I don't really like the way my life looks when I look around and see everything I've neglected."

"Oh?"

"I guess I handle things differently than my husband, where I kind of withdrew into myself."

"You always were thoughtful and contemplative. The creative types sometimes have a tendency to be manic depressive almost. Not that you are, but periods of great and wild creativity, followed by periods of depression or, in your case, contemplation and thoughtfulness."

She hadn't seen that about herself before, and it was interesting that Mrs. Calvin had.

"He threw himself into his work to keep busy."

"And that's how he handles things. He needs to work with his hands, to get his mind off of the stuff. When he's thinking, he has to be working. That's the way my Ike is. He's a man of the Word, but a lot of times, he read the Word while he was standing up in his study, maybe lifting a weight, or pacing in front of the window. He would sit down if he had to write, but he liked to be moving."

"I remember that about him. He always had some kind of project he was doing. Either at the church or at your home."

"Yeah. I miss all the fun little additions he made that personalized our home into something beautiful. It was a one-of-a-kind place."

"The new couple who bought it seem really sweet. They sit on the porch a good bit, and I haven't talked to them as much as I would like to."

She hadn't done anything as much as she would like to lately.

"They seemed like a really nice couple, just retired, so our house is perfect for them. But you were telling me about your life and how you emerged from your recovery from losing your son, and things aren't exactly what you wanted them to be."

"No. They're not. I told you that my husband threw himself into work."

"Yes. And you didn't, so...you drifted apart?"

Of course she would guess. "Yes. Exactly. And I'm not quite sure how to get back together. It feels hard."

"Relationships are hard. But you might as well face it head-on. Both of you want to get back together and figure out how to reignite what you had or how to move forward with how you've grown and changed. Correct?"

"I'm not sure. I guess it's sad that I've let things get so far away from me that I really don't even know."

Mrs. Calvin gazed out the window, but Vera figured she probably didn't see the view of the parking lot. "Well, you haven't asked me for advice, but I would say that's your first step. You need to make sure that you're both on the same page. And then, once you know that both of you want the same things, you can figure out how to get them."

"I suppose that's true. Except..."

Could she tell Mrs. Calvin about Shoshana? They were just suspicions. Hearsay. Maybe she could present them like that.

"My husband decided to work with another designer while I was not working."

Her eyes widened, and she gasped. "He did?"

Her reaction soothed Vera's soul just a little. So it wasn't just her. Other people, people who were close to them, expected them to only work with each other.

"Yeah. A competitor of mine, but a friendly one. We're not enemies or anything."

"But still, another designer is...almost like aiding and abetting the enemy."

Vera laughed. It wasn't that bad. At least...she didn't think so.

"Not like that, except..." She stopped, looking out the window at the beautiful green grass and the flowers that grew on the edge of the parking lot. Vera supposed the lake-view suites were probably more expensive, and Pastor and his wife could not afford one.

Drawing her attention back to the subject at hand, she said, "I wouldn't say aiding and abetting the enemy because she's my competitor, not my enemy, but I don't know what the relationship is, and I'm not sure how to figure it out."

"How about you ask your husband?"

"Yeah. That's probably what I ought to do, except, if there's something going on, he's going to deny it, right? And if there isn't anything going on, he's going to deny it. So, I'm expecting him to deny it or else say 'yes, there's something going on and I want a divorce.'"

Mrs. Calvin flinched at the use of the D word. "Is your woman's intuition telling you that there's something going on?"

"I don't know. I don't really trust myself anymore. I just feel like I woke up one day and all of a sudden nothing was the way it used to be, and I realize that most of it's my fault because I've been out of life for so long."

She didn't know how else to explain it.

"I see. It does kind of throw you for a loop when you come up for air and you realize that life has gone on without you, and things you thought you knew aren't necessarily what you thought they were anymore."

"Yeah. That's a good explanation, and I don't know what to do about it. I don't know how to ask my husband and know he's not lying to me."

"But he's never made a habit of lying to you."

"I've never seen him lie, ever. Not even to make someone feel good. You know? Like he wouldn't give a compliment if he didn't mean it. Today he told me I was beautiful, and it took me aback because I know he wouldn't just say that. He wouldn't tell me something he didn't truly mean."

"So then you can ask him and expect the truth, except if a man is cheating, that already goes against the character and integrity that he usually displays, so maybe he would start a new habit of lying." Mrs. Calvin sighed. "I would say, if you don't have any concrete evidence, you have to assume the best."

"That's what I decided as well."

"It doesn't hurt to keep an eye out for things that are not quite right, and if you have a feeling that they might not be, I wouldn't discount that. But like you said, it might just be because you haven't been around for a while. Or it might be because you're already a little jealous that he was working with your competitor."

"I thought of that. Like, it might be just me. Just me making these things up. Blowing everything out of proportion because he hurt my feelings. I don't want to be like that."

Fourteen

"Well, good. It's good that you know it. And I guess the only thing you can do is pray about it and then decide that you're going to believe the best about your husband, no matter what. And if he wants to stay with you and work with you to rebuild your relationship, I would say..." Mrs. Calvin paused for a moment, her eyes narrowing as her cheeks wrinkled, and her gnarled finger came up and tapped her nose. "I don't mean to say that cheating isn't a big thing, it is. But he might have been lonely and upset, and I'm not trying to justify it, but he might have made a mistake. A big one. A massive mistake. But still, just a mistake."

She thought maybe Mrs. Calvin was telling her that if her husband cheated on her, then she needed to forgive him. Especially if he wanted to continue the relationship and heal their marriage.

It made sense. If her husband wanted to work on their marriage, wanted to stay in it, wanted to get back what they had, she should be able to forgive him for a mistake.

She just didn't know if she was that mature.

"I'd like to be able to do that. It makes sense in my head, but the feminine part of me... I want to be someone's one and only. I don't want to be his, 'as long as you're paying attention to me, I'll be true to you, but as soon as something bad happens and you withdraw into yourself to handle it, I'm going to go find the first available woman who's ready to go to bed with me' person."

She knew she was being a little bit snide, and Mrs. Calvin flinched again.

"Sorry. I guess—"

"You're hurt. You're hurt, and you're lashing out. Which makes sense from a human perspective. It's what we do. But animals do it too. And animals don't have the ability to rationalize and figure out that maybe what they're doing isn't a good idea. And they don't have the ability to have self-control and decide that they're going to do something different, something Jesus wants them to do, rather than what they want to do themselves. I suppose that's why we're made in God's image and animals are not. That's what makes humans special." Mrs. Calvin shook her head. "And that's why evolution is so dangerous, because it puts us all in the same field. We're all the same according to the 'science.' But we're not. God made humans special. We're not the same as animals, and as much as I loved my pets over the years, they were not humans, and I think we're losing out a little bit in our society."

Maybe Mrs. Calvin was talking just to give her a chance to think without being obvious about the necessity of just needing some time to process.

She wasn't an animal. She didn't have to react the way she felt. She could control herself. She could think about things and come to a rational conclusion and make her behavior follow suit. And she could even think about things and come to a conclusion that wasn't rational, but was hard, and almost impossible, but commanded by Jesus, and therefore she could do it. Through Him.

She pulled her lips in, biting down.

"I wish I could help you. I wish I could take that pain. I can see your struggle, but I think it's kind of like a butterfly. You need to struggle. You need the pain. Whatever God is trying to mold you into, you have to go through this, and, you have to go through it with the right attitude, with the goal of being more like Jesus, not with the goal of making sure that everybody gets what's coming to them, making sure people pay for what they've done. Your job is not other people. Your job is you."

It was Mrs. Calvin's turn to put a little snark in her words so that she almost sounded less like a pastor's wife and more like a modern woman who was demanding she get everything that she deserved.

It wasn't biblical at all. It didn't show strength. It showed the mental capacity of a two-year-old throwing a temper tantrum.

Mrs. Calvin couldn't tell her what to do, she could only offer suggestions and guide her according to God's word. It was up to Vera to make the decisions that would save her marriage or save her pride.

Did she have to choose between the two of them?

Actually, she shouldn't. Her pride shouldn't even be in contention. She wasn't supposed to have any. So, that should make the decision easy. Except, she wanted to hold onto it with both hands and demand her husband treat her the way she deserved and not the way it looked like he had.

But Mrs. Calvin was right about one thing. She had to believe the best about her husband. If she didn't start doing better at that, she was going to drive herself crazy.

They started talking about the church in Raspberry Ridge, and how Mrs. Calvin had not expected for it to stay closed for so long, and how she hoped that someone was going to come along and open it, and rebuild the congregation.

"Maybe we need a committee or something, since I haven't heard a thing about it. Of course, you know that I've been a little under the weather."

"But you're coming out of it now. And...maybe I shouldn't say this, because I never said anything to his mother, but do you know Homer Aitken?"

"Sure do. Of course. He went to church, but he also lives right at the end of Raspberry Ridge. There's a garden and a garage along the road before the road ends and the little patch of ground starts where Dominic and I are going to construct our memory garden."

"I want to hear more about that memory garden, but I always thought Homer would make a good preacher."

"I loved to go to Sunday school and listen to what he said. He wasn't the teacher, but he always had such good insight into Scripture."

"I thought he was blessed in that area, too. Now, God calls preachers, men don't, and women don't either." Mrs. Calvin laughed. "But if I were calling a preacher, Homer would be on my list."

"Maybe God called him, but he couldn't answer because he was taking care of his mother. Did you hear that she has early-onset Alzheimer's?"

"No," Mrs. Calvin said, the word kind of going down in a sad, 'I can't believe that, I'm so disappointed about that' kind of way.

"Yeah. She visited me not that long ago, and she has such a great attitude about it. It was so inspiring. I only hope that I'm able to be like that if I get a diagnosis like that. She just...accepted it, and she doesn't seem regretful or sad at all."

"I always admired Gertie's walk with the Lord. Sometimes I thought that rather than marrying the surgeon, she should have married a pastor. She would have made an excellent pastor's wife."

"That's a hard job. You have people like me, confiding in you all the time, and you have to take all of the terrible things you hear every day, and put them aside, and still have a happy, positive attitude."

"Not to mention all the criticism I hear about my husband. Sometimes I wanted to go to him so bad and tell him who said what, but I just didn't see how that would do anybody any good. I prayed about it instead."

"I think that was smart. God can handle it," Vera said. "Maybe that's what I should do. Just pray."

"I think you'll find that God doesn't take away your troubles immediately. And He doesn't work everything out magically, but if you pray, God will move. Believe it."

The door opened then, and the men walked in.

"We need to go outside more, Edna May. It's beautiful out."

"What in the world would I do if you fell?" Edna May said gently. "We both know I couldn't get you back up."

"That's why we came here. There are call bells in every room. You could jump into somebody's room and hit their call button. Then, when people come to that room, you just intercept them and say it's you that needs help for your husband."

"I suppose I could, but I'd rather not have you fall to begin with. I don't want anything to happen to you."

"Well, I think even when we were younger, we knew that we couldn't live our lives from a place of fear, wondering if anything was going to happen. We need to live it from a position of faith. Trusting that God will keep us safe, and when He doesn't, it's not time for us to be safe. It's time for us to be brave."

Mrs. Calvin smiled as she and Vera rose to their feet. She looked at Vera. "How can I not have faith, when I have such inspiration in my husband."

"That was a good, inspiring speech. I think I could use that. It was almost better than an hour-long sermon."

Pastor Calvin laughed. "Sometimes I think I could have shortened my sermons by about ninety-nine percent and people would have gotten the same amount out of them. However, I was always afraid that if I did that, the deacon board would suggest that they cut my pay by ninety-nine percent as well. I wasn't quite willing to take that risk, bravery or no."

Vera grinned again, and her eyes moved to Dominic. Maybe they were pulled there, but she saw him smiling as well and looking fondly at the old pastor.

Sometimes it was sad that time had to go on, things had to change, people had to get old, children had to die.

On the one hand, she wished she could rewind time and go back ten years, back to when they were happy. When Pastor and Mrs. Calvin served faithfully in church, old but not elderly, when she and Dominic had a strong and robust relationship, and when the promise of a child loomed almost on the horizon.

It felt like that time was much better than this time, but she supposed ten years from now, she'd look back on this time with longing as well.

Actually, she doubted it. This seemed like one of those dark times in her life that she would never want to revisit, not for anything.

They said goodbye to the pastor and his wife, and Dominic opened the door for her, and she walked out.

"Would you like to stop at the snack shop and grab an ice cream or something? It really is a pretty view out front, and I feel bad that Pastor and Mrs. Calvin have rooms on the other side. Pastor told me that the rooms with the view are almost double in price, and there is a waiting list for them as well."

"That makes sense. But it's too bad. Although I guess it doesn't really matter to Pastor whether there's a view or not."

"No. He told me that he can still see shapes sometimes, but he really can't see, for example, a stone or something on the floor so that he can move and not trip over it. Or he can't distinguish people by their facial features. He has to hear their voice."

"He did a good job of recognizing mine. He knew me as soon as I spoke."

"Me too. I think sometimes when one sense is affected, our other senses are sharpened. It's sad that the sense you're losing couldn't be sharpened by extra work or something. You know? Like, if your hearing can become better because your eyesight fails, why can't you put cotton in your ears and practice looking at things, to help your eyesight come better?"

"I never thought of that. That's a good point," Vera said as they automatically started walking toward the snack shop.

She hadn't said yes to his request, but she hadn't needed to. She supposed her walking in that direction was all he needed.

"It's kind of odd that they put a snack shop up on the second floor, isn't it?"

"Don't they have one on the bottom, too?" she asked.

"I suppose they do. I guess it's fair, a snack shop for each floor. The delivery guy has to walk further to stock this one."

"Maybe there's a place around back for him to drop things off."

That was the kind of thing they might have talked about years ago, just different things that they thought of and discussed. He would give his opinion, and she might give a little bit of insight he hadn't thought about. Or she might do the same, have an opinion about something, and he might challenge it a little. Not in a competitive or unkind way, but in the kind of way that being with another person shapes and grows you, challenges you to think a little bit differently than what you're used to thinking or what you're prone to think.

She missed that in her life. Maybe that was why it took her so long to get over the death of her son. She didn't have her husband near her challenging her, inspiring her, trying to show her a different way to think.

She was just thinking about slipping her hand into his when his phone rang.

He smiled apologetically and grabbed his phone out of his pocket. She expected him to silence the ring and put it back. That's kind of how he'd been acting lately, and it was what he used to do when they were together.

His lips pinched back.

"I ought to take this." He held his phone up, shifting it back and forth, like he was waving it, which was enough for her to see the name that came up with the number.

Shoshana.

She jerked her head. "We can get ice cream some other time."

His brow wrinkled, but he had already swiped on his phone to answer, and he put it to his ear, still looking at her like he wanted to argue.

But she turned and started walking toward the elevator.

She was supposed to think the best of him. She was supposed to think the best of him. She tried to remind herself as she silently chanted she was supposed to think the best of him.

She could hear his voice rumbling in the background. It sounded like he hadn't moved. Did he not want to be in the elevator with her while he was on the phone with Shoshana?

That must have been what he intended, since she reached the elevator, and he wasn't behind her.

Pushing the button, she tried to decide whether she would get on and go down without him.

When the elevator dinged, and the empty car opened, she walked on, turning around, unable to see her husband, who was still back at the snack shop, down the hall and around the corner.

Well, she was on, and she wasn't going to just stand there, so she pushed the button for the first floor, and the doors closed.

Fifteen

Dominic hurried down the hall, looking around. He couldn't see her anywhere.

He should have followed her when she left, but he was still thinking he would get ice cream, and they would eat it together. It seemed like a nice little ending to what wasn't exactly a date; visiting the old folks' home was not exactly an idea of a romantic getaway, but they both enjoyed talking to their old pastor and his wife. And even if they didn't enjoy it, he felt like they had brightened their day a little, and that gave him a better feeling than almost anything else he could have done. Other than spend time with his wife.

Regardless, ice cream would be the topper, except...Vera had walked off like she was upset about something.

That was odd, but he hurried around the corner, thinking maybe she was waiting at the elevator, and they could still go back for ice cream, but she wasn't there.

Nor was she waiting in the living area downstairs, nor the reception area near the doors. He didn't see her until he stepped out into the bright sunlight, sitting on a bench by the water fountain. It wasn't any great work of art, nothing like she could design or he could build, but it gave the trickling sound of water, which was relaxing at any time, and it was enjoyable to watch.

It didn't run in the winter of course, but at night, they had colored lights that lit up and changed and were really pretty. He'd seen it when they first moved Pastor and Mrs. Calvin into the assisted living center.

He started to walk over toward his wife, but a sound caught his attention, and he looked up, shielding his face from the sun.

Was that a helicopter?

It sounded like a helicopter, and then as he looked back over at his wife, he saw about six or seven cars that pulled into the assisted living center parking lot at that time.

It felt like a lot of things were happening at once, as the helicopter grew closer and closer.

Dominic strode over to his wife, who had stood up from the bench and looked first at the cars, then at the helicopter.

"I think it's going to land here," she said with surprise.

He looked up, realizing the helicopter was getting closer and closer and seemed to be aiming for the back area of the parking lot, which was completely devoid of cars.

The cars that had just pulled in seemed to be parked over in that general direction.

"Was something supposed to happen here today?" Vera asked, drawing her brows down.

"I'm pretty sure that if there was, Pastor and Mrs. Calvin would have mentioned it."

He wasn't sure which one of them started moving first, but he soon found that Vera and he were walking across the parking lot, his hand on the small of her back, toward the helicopter which indeed had landed. As they watched, a gentleman with dark shades and a white dog trailing him stepped down.

It looked like a fancy helicopter, black and sleek, and to their surprise, there was a whole gaggle of people standing there waiting for the man, some of them yelling his name and some of them throwing things at him. Undergarments, it looked like.

A big, burly man stepped out behind the first man and spread his arms wide, forming a barrier beside him with his arms, getting him through the gaggle of ladies.

The man continued to stride forward, confidence in his walk, although a little bit of confusion on his face. Somehow, Dominic wasn't even surprised to see the lab frolic at the man's heels, sauntering past the ladies, trotting behind the man.

Finally, the man reached Dominic and Vera and held out his hand. "Good morning! I'm Jay Dyess. With whom do I have the pleasure of speaking?"

Dominic shook the man's hand, even though the whole scene seemed a little off. "I'm Dominic Miller, and this is my wife, Vera. We weren't expecting to see a helicopter land in the parking lot of the Blueberry Beach nursing home."

"This is a nursing home?" Jay said.

"Yes," Dominic said, realizing it was obvious the man wasn't expecting to land at a nursing home but not sure how to help him.

"So there's no romance convention going on here today?" Jay finally said, looking around the parking lot and then back over his shoulder.

"No. Sorry," Dominic said, shrugging his shoulders.

Jay's lips pressed together, and he shook his head, although he didn't seem too put out. "Man, Jessie gave me the wrong directions. Again."

He sighed, reached into his pocket, and pulled out a small slip of paper and handed it to Dominic. "That's my dad's BBQ chicken recipe. Consider it a little thank you for your trouble."

Shaking his head again, he lifted a hand in farewell, turned abruptly, and strode back toward the helicopter, his bodyguard making sure the ladies who gathered around didn't press too tightly or get close enough to touch Mr. Dyess.

"Was that *the* Jay Dyess?" Vera asked.

"That's who he said he was."

"The famous narrator."

"Yes. I've never seen him before, but I did recognize his voice. He's the famous narrator who was reading the story that Pastor and Mrs. Calvin were listening to as we walked in."

"Yeah, I recognized his voice too, but I didn't realize he had a helicopter and a whole entourage," he said as he watched first Mr. Dyess get in the helicopter, and then his dog jumped after him. "If I'd have realized who it was, I would have asked for an autograph. But it's not like the outside of the helicopter says anything."

"No. That's too bad. I would have liked his autograph, and I know Mrs. Calvin would have really enjoyed it as well."

They stood in silence as the helicopter took off. The gaggle of ladies got back in their cars and took off in the same direction as the helicopter did.

"I bet the convention is in Chicago."

"I don't know. I wonder who the Jessie was that he was talking about?" Vera asked.

Dominic shrugged. "I have no idea. His administrative assistant or travel agent, I suppose." He looked off in the distance at the helicopter as it disappeared. "It seems like wherever he goes, he has a whole fan club following him. Must be interesting to be so famous."

Vera put her arms around her waist, and they started back toward their car. It made him wonder if she had wanted to be that famous.

"Would you like to be famous like that?"

"And ride around in a helicopter?" She laughed. "I suppose that would be a fun way to get around. Then you wouldn't have to worry about rush-hour traffic. But I've never wanted to be famous on my own. I just wanted to design the very best that I could and see them come to life, giving people rest and comfort."

"Yeah." And that was something he had always admired about her. She had been fine with the two of them getting a lot of attention, but she hadn't wanted to draw attention to herself just for the sake of making her name big.

Unlike Shoshana. She wouldn't quit pestering him about doing another project with her. The stipulation for her to get the design contract was that he agreed to build it, and as she kept trying to tell him, it was for one of the biggest film studios in California. They would have star-power, Hollywood names begging them to work for them, and they might even eventually get a star on the Walk of Fame according to her. Whatever that was.

She didn't understand that none of that interested him at all.

Unfortunately, the camaraderie and the few small steps he seemed to have taken toward repairing his relationship with his wife seemed to have disappeared, or maybe they'd gone backward. Vera was quiet on the way home and answered his questions with yes or no or a shrug of her shoulders.

When they got home, she went directly to the sunroom and pulled her laptop open.

He had talked to Pastor, and Pastor had told him that he needed to romance his wife. Even when a man was married, he needed to romance her, and in fact, Pastor had said that a lot of times, the romance should happen after the marriage, not before.

A man needed to give his best efforts after he had won his wife, because keeping a marriage fresh, keeping it strong, staying together, and appreciating each other were things that a man needed to work on after the wedding day.

Pastor had winked and said there were other things that a man needed to work on after the wedding day as well, and it made Dominic laugh, although they hadn't talked about that any more.

He hadn't romanced his wife in a long time. And he had no one to blame for the rift that was between them but himself. He wished Shoshana hadn't called and interrupted what wasn't exactly a date with his wife, but everything seemed to go downhill after that.

He wondered why. What happened? Had something Mrs. Calvin said upset her?

He tried to think back, but he wasn't in the room. He couldn't know. But what would it have been? Was she thinking about Trent again?

Maybe they just needed to face the Trent thing head-on.

He pulled his phone out and texted his wife. I thought I'd go see Trent's grave tomorrow. Want to come?

Her answer took about a minute to come back. Sure. We'll leave at ten?

Yes.

That was definitely not a date, but maybe that was the thing that was between them that needed to be settled. He couldn't think of anything else. Unless...she was just tired of him. Maybe seeing a famous voice actor like Jay Dyess had reminded her that she was just married to a simple man, someone who worked with his hands for a living, who didn't have helicopters or gaggles of women following him around, tossing their undergarments at him, and swooning every time he lifted his fingers.

He didn't even have a handsome dog.

He could fix the issue about the dog, but he wouldn't get a dog without his wife's approval.

Maybe seeing someone like that had made Vera realize that she didn't have anyone special, and she could have done a lot better.

But she'd gone down in the elevator without him, and that had been before she'd seen Mr. Dyess.

Was it because he took the phone call rather than silencing it?

Maybe he shouldn't have. For most people, he wouldn't have, but Shoshana was a well-known designer, and being associated with her might help Vera's career, if she ever decided she wanted to have a career again. He hadn't wanted to close every door with her, because he wanted to make sure that Vera had every advantage possible. It had excited him to think that Vera's career might take off because he had introduced her to the top designer in the nation. Vera could design circles around Shoshana, she just needed the opportunity.

Shoshana had more opportunity and more luck than Vera ever would. Shoshana came from money, she'd never had children, and she didn't have a husband or home, as she'd divorced two husbands. Obviously she didn't spend a lot of time taking care of them.

He shouldn't think such things about her. Maybe she put every effort into her marriages, and they just hadn't worked out. Regardless, he had been excited that Vera might be able to move up in the world, because of Shoshana. And he hadn't wanted to brush her off, even though he didn't want to work with her again.

Sure, it had been a good thing for his career, with just a few downsides. It made it seem like he was available for any designer, and not all designers were created equal. His wife just got him. They thought on the same level, they created on the same plane, their creations complemented each other, while he didn't feel that at all while working with Shoshana, and he thought their completed project reflected that.

He'd made enough money, he didn't need to work with her, and... he'd rather be with his wife.

But he didn't see her the rest of the day, and when he heard the water running for her to take a shower, he grabbed a bite to eat, thinking maybe they would have a chance to talk before she went to bed. But she was in bed, curled up on her side, clear over on the edge, when he walked in.

He said her name softly, but she didn't answer.

Going into the bathroom, he took his own shower, deciding that he'd get up and watch the sunrise with her in the morning, and they'd go see Trent's grave together. Plus, she'd see what he'd finally done. He smiled at the thought. Tomorrow was going to be a good day.

Sixteen

Vera lay in bed, wide awake at four AM, wondering whether she should get up and go down to the sunroom and avoid her husband as much as she could.

But she knew that wasn't the right thing to do. She needed to figure things out, and they needed to talk. She'd been putting it off long enough. Of course, going to Trent's grave might not be the best place to discuss Shoshana, and...she needed to think the best of him.

And she had been upset the day before when Shoshana called and he answered it like it was important or something. And she just didn't know whether she could be kind to him and not come off like a shrew and bring up Shoshana, in a tone of voice no woman should use with her husband.

Rather than yelling at him and being angry, she knew it was best for her to just take a little bit of time, calm down, and wait until she could be decent before she reached out, hoping that they could work things out.

Deciding that she would get up and watch the sunrise, because she was already awake, and because she needed to meet him halfway, just in case he did, she got out of bed and got dressed.

He was still snoring, and she thought that he might not make it up.

But as the horizon started to turn deep, burnt orange, and she sat on her chair, the door opened, and he walked up behind her.

She was snuggled in her blanket like she usually was, her cup of coffee held in both hands.

"Good morning, beautiful."

He said good morning, and she could have handled it, but he added the beautiful onto it, and she closed her eyes.

Lord, I don't think I can do this. I'm gonna fall in love with my husband, and then I'm going to find out terrible things, and it's going to break me.

But somehow, after praying the prayer, she was reminded that Jesus allowed himself to be wrecked. He allowed it. And he believed in the goodness of mankind, even when he knew how sinful and wicked they were. How prone to evil constantly, but he was always holding out a hand, offering love and forgiveness and redemption, all she had to do was take it.

Could she do the same to her husband?

"Good morning," she said in a voice that didn't quite sound like hers.

Typically they didn't talk a whole lot, and this morning was no different, but as he walked behind her, his hand trailed along a strand of her hair, touching her shoulder.

They used to have little touches like that all the time. And she loved it. Touch wasn't necessarily her love language, but she loved his touch on her hair, feeling his fingers in it, or just one finger twirling it around, absently, or with that lopsided grin on his face, watching her, touching her, feeling connected through that touch that wasn't sexual at all, just... something that bonded two people together.

Her breath felt a little wobbly until he walked away, standing at the railing for a bit, before he walked to the other side. Typical for him, only he didn't seem to be as deep in thought as he usually was.

"I backed out of three of the four contracts that I had coming, and I withdrew my bid from everything that I had bid on in the last several months."

"Okay," she said, interested but more interested in why Shoshana was calling him. She held her breath, wondering if he was going to tell her, or if it was something that she was going to end up wondering about for the rest of her life.

No. She would be talking to him about it. But not now. Not unless he brought it up.

They didn't typically talk business in the morning though, and he didn't say anything more. Rather, he walked over to the far banister, leaning against it, his eyes on the sunrise rather than the lake area.

It was like he was shifting his focus.

She didn't want to read anything more into it than what he meant.

The sunrise wasn't quite as glorious that morning, because of some low-hanging clouds, and it was over quickly, unlike some sunrises which seemed to last for an hour or more.

She stood. "We're still going to the cemetery?" She didn't know why she couldn't say Trent's grave to her husband. She'd spoken her son's name multiple times and had gotten good at doing it without starting to cry.

"10 o'clock?"

That seemed to be their time of launch, even though they were both up well before then.

"Yes."

"I ran out and bought some flowers. They're in the carport. I thought we'd plant them. It's not too early, is it?"

"No. It's the perfect time."

The safe frost date had passed, and it was the perfect time to plant flowers on his grave. She wondered what color he had gotten. She had always bought geraniums for the grave, she wasn't quite sure why. Red ones.

But red was not Trent's favorite color. He preferred blue. Every once in a while, he would say it was brown or black.

That would make her cringe a little, hoping that he outgrew that. Not that there was anything wrong with anyone who had a favorite color of black, just it wasn't her favorite color or even close to it.

It reminded her of death.

Regardless, she walked into the house, taking her coffee cup with her and going to the sunroom.

She was able to get a little bit further on her design, although it wasn't nearly finished and she appreciated the fact that Dominic was not pushing her on it.

She had noticed that the bulldozer was there yesterday when they were on their way home, but unless he'd run it some when he'd gone to pick up flowers, she thought maybe he would be doing it today.

She hadn't even noticed he left.

Still, at 9:45, she put her things away and thought she might go upstairs and freshen up a bit. She wasn't going to change into anything nice, especially if she was going to be on her hands and knees planting flowers for her son.

When she planted them before, she looked carefully at some of the gravestones and found four other children that were buried there, having lived and died from thirty years ago to more than one hundred. She had no idea who they were, but she had bought four extra flowers and decorated their graves as well. Anyone who was going to remember them or take care of them had probably long passed away, and it just seemed sad for a child's grave to not have some kind of decoration on it. Some kind of little touch that said *I love you. And you're missed.*

Maybe it wouldn't matter when she was dead and gone. There would be no one to take care of her grave anyway.

But before she could leave the sunroom, the phone rang. It was Peggy, and she smiled.

"Hey there," she answered, pushing her hair back and smiling as she stretched her legs, walking around the small room, looking out the windows. "I'm leaving in fifteen minutes to go see Trent's grave with Dominic, so I don't have a lot of time."

"Hello to you too, and thanks for letting me know. I really didn't want anything." Peggy paused. "So, you and Dominic...?" She let her voice trail off, with a little question at the end.

Vera sighed, long and deep, and loud enough for Peggy to hear.

"Still not good?"

"I don't know. I just... I don't know. But how are you?"

"Oh, I'm doing good. I think I'm gonna change my nail color. I've been wearing it for three days now, and I've decided I don't like it."

"Oh, you should get a happy turquoise, or turquoise and pink. That says spring."

"That's a good idea. This is red, and I think it makes me look old."

"You don't look old, Peggy." Vera laughed, loving that they could talk about something frivolous and completely irrelevant to life, and not have to be so emotional all the time.

"I just want to check up on you and make sure that you are okay. Also... I wanted to know if you have someone going with you to the tenth anniversary party. If you don't, you know I'm in."

"Actually, I think Dominic is going. He asked me if I was and reminded me that we had tickets. So, I think you're off the hook for this one."

"You know I love seeing you. And, Pittsburgh isn't a bad city, especially this time of year. It'll be pretty. All that water and those rivers and the spring flowers everywhere."

"I think that's why they decided to have the celebration now, just because the blooms of the garden should be beautiful." She had planned it so that there were flowers blooming in every season, except winter of course. Since no flowers grew in Pittsburgh in the winter. But she kept that in mind too and tried to plan the grasses and trees so that even bare, they would form some kind of artistic impression, even though she obviously couldn't determine exactly how trees grew.

"Hey, girl, schedule me in sometime for a long chat, okay?"

There was something about what she said that triggered something in Vera's mind, and she hesitated just a moment before she said, "You know I will. We'll plan on it. I'll send you a text."

They hung up, and Vera stood there for a moment. And then she realized what the nagging idea was.

The scheduling app that she and Dominic shared that showed nothing on it for Shoshana. She hadn't thought to check to see if Dominic had added Shoshana onto the calendar. No one else had eyes on it other than Dominic and Vera, and they just kept their business appointments there, but...she didn't know why that idea came to her, but he might have. If he was having an affair with her, she'd need to know what his schedule was.

Glancing at the clock, she saw it was 9:58. Later than she would usually start to head outside, so she resisted the urge to open her laptop and go directly to the scheduling app.

She could check it out later.

It took a lot of self-control to make herself walk out the door of the sunroom, and it took even more self-control to pull her mind from that idea. She should have checked, then she wouldn't be wondering about it this entire time.

As it was, it was going to be hard to get her mind off that, but she was in control of her thoughts. She didn't have to think about whether Shoshana had been added as a viewer or admin to their schedule, she didn't have to think about the what-ifs. She reminded herself of that and was able to give her husband a pleased smile as she walked outside and saw him waiting at the front of his truck.

Seventeen

Vera took another step toward the truck before she saw it. The flower boxes that she had asked him to make were put together and placed on the retaining wall that they had built on the side of the driveway.

Dominic had made them, placed them, filled them with soil, and planted flowers yesterday afternoon sometime after they came home or early this morning.

They were blooming profusely and looked exactly the way she had pictured it when she had designed it.

She had asked him to do that. In fact, it was the last thing she had asked him to do before Trent had passed away.

She thought maybe he would do it while she was mourning, to keep his hands busy and to make her feel better, but he hadn't.

She pushed that thought aside. She had to, or it would make her bitter. She would wonder why he couldn't have done that instead of partner with Shoshana if he wanted to keep his hands busy.

Let it go. Just push it aside, and focus on how wonderful your husband is.

She allowed the big smile that she wanted to pop out to cover her face.

"Look what you did yesterday. Wow, you were busy. And it looks amazing," she said, allowing their eyes to meet, for him to see how happy she was, before she looked back, going down the rest of the stairs and walking over to the short stone wall.

There wasn't much of a hill in their yard, but the retaining wall kept the dirt aside and was almost level with the ground there, and it gave the driveway a sunken look. Now framed by flowers, it was beautiful.

"I've been thinking about that for a while, and..." He cleared his throat. "I think I got addicted to being busy. Or addicted to success in my business or something."

She didn't say anything. Is that what it was? It wasn't...someone else?

She hated that her brain went there. Dragging it back, she kept the smile on her face and in her eyes as she turned back to him. "You made it look better than I pictured it. When I designed it, I thought it was going to look good, but just how you put it all together, it looks amazing."

That he could read her mind, that he could know what she wanted and be able to put it together so effortlessly, always amazed her. His work was the same as everyone else's, yet different. Just different enough that it seemed to bring out whatever her design needed, and... She couldn't quite put her finger on it, but she stood back and then looked over at him with her arms crossed over her chest.

"Thank you. This is amazing."

"You're not angry that I gave you more work to do? You have flowers to water now?"

"You know I live for those kinds of things," she said, smiling at him, as the knowledge that she was right went over his face and his smile broadened a little.

They grinned at each other, and something passed between them. Something that felt familiar, yet lost. Maybe something they could find together.

She was ready to drop her arms and walk toward him, the way she would have before, but his phone rang.

A bit of irritation crossed his face, and that almost made her smile grow bigger. Maybe he didn't want to be interrupted when he was with her.

But it vanished, and he pulled his phone out of his pocket, glancing at it before shoving it back in.

The moment was broken though, and although she looked at the planters again, she started walking toward her side of the pickup.

He hurried around, putting his hand on the small of her back for two strides, before he reached around and opened her door.

"Thank you," she murmured, appreciating the fact that he was making the effort. Obviously, he was making the effort. And she wasn't going to have any suspicions about it. She refused to allow those thoughts into her brain.

She turned to give him a smile and saw that he was still standing at her door, his head leaning in a little.

"Sorry I didn't do it sooner," he said softly, his words almost like a caress.

"It's water under the bridge. I appreciate it now."

The apology made it so much easier to accept. It made it easier for her to brush aside the fact that he was working with Shoshana instead of making planters for her after their son died.

It was okay. It really was, and maybe it was a mistake on his part. She could forget mistakes. She could overlook the fact that maybe it wasn't the best thing that he could have done, but...she hadn't done the best thing either. She completely neglected her husband and hadn't felt a single bit bad about it. She just wanted to fall in on herself and curl up in the coffin beside Trent.

She hadn't been thinking about Dominic at all, how could she be upset that he wasn't thinking about her?

Except she wasn't dealing with her grief by working with some other man.

He had given her another long look before he jerked his chin up, which meant he accepted her words, although maybe he had other things to say about them, but he didn't know how to put his thoughts into words at the moment.

He closed her door, and she finished putting her seat belt on.

They didn't talk on the way to the cemetery, which wasn't a long ride, and it wasn't an awkward silence, like the one yesterday had been.

It was a contemplative silence. Maybe both of them were

remembering how spring meant T-ball and baseball and boating and fishing and exploring along the beach.

Trent's curiosity was insatiable, and long before school was out, he wanted to go to the beach, to find the perfect pebbles, and then as he grew older, to hunt for treasure, and fish and find small crustaceans.

Those he wanted to eat, and it was one of the few times that Vera had said, "You're going to have to talk to your father about that."

She smiled at the memory.

"I can't believe you're smiling," Dominic said as they pulled into the cemetery.

She turned eyes to him that maybe held sadness but still held humor too. "I was remembering about Trent and his crustaceans. He wanted to eat them. I don't even know whether you guys ever did, but it was one of the few things that I said that you were going to have to handle."

"You did a good job with him when I wasn't around."

"You tried to be here as much as you could." He wasn't gone much. Maybe two weeks total all summer long.

"It was more than I wanted to be. I wanted to spend every second of every day with the two of you."

"Same. My whole world was complete when I was with my men."

Her statement made him smile, but it was a sad smile as well. "You ready?"

She nodded. He got out with her. She walked around to the back of the truck, where she assumed he had his flowers and shovel, and she was correct. There was also a bucket of manure and a bucket with a lid filled with water.

"You want to look at it first?" he asked. "Before I carry all the stuff over?"

She saw he had four extra flowers.

She looked at them for a minute, and then she said, "What were you going to do with these four extras?"

"Remember how you planted flowers at the other kids' graves?"

She smiled. She hadn't expected him to remember. But he did. It warmed her the whole way through to her bones that he had taken what she had done, and internalized it, remembered it a year later, and had bought enough flowers to do it again.

He hadn't needed to remember. She wouldn't have been angry or upset. But the fact that he did showed her he cared, truly cared about her, more than anything else he could have done.

"I... That means a lot to me—"

His phone started to ring, shrill in the quiet of the cemetery. They were far enough away from the lake that they couldn't see the blue vastness from where they were but could still feel the light breeze and see the huge sky.

And now, the solitude was shattered by the metallic ringtone.

His mouth flattened again, as though irritated, as he pulled it from his pocket and looked at it.

He shook his head, silenced it, and shoved it back in his pocket. "Sorry about that."

"Somebody really wants you," she said, giving him an opening if he wanted to tell her about Shoshana. But telling herself not to hold her breath. She would get to the bottom of it, but this wasn't the time.

"They're going to have to wait. I'm with my wife right now. And we're going to plant some flowers on my son and his friends' graves."

That's exactly how she had thought about it! But she knew she hadn't told him because it was...not only impossible, but a little silly. She knew that the kids in the graveyard weren't even close to her son's age, weren't his contemporaries, were old enough to be his great-grandparents, they wouldn't play together ever, and they probably wouldn't have understood each other if they could have talked to each other, coming from different decades, even different centuries.

But it made her feel good that there was a group of kids in the graveyard, all having flowers together.

"I've often wanted to come back, just to make sure I didn't miss any. I found four that day. But afterward, I felt like if I missed one, they might not feel like they're part of the group, which is ridiculous." She knew it was, and she closed her eyes. Then she opened them again. "You said it. So, maybe I don't sound quite so ridiculous to you?"

"You never sound ridiculous to me. And yeah, today, or if that doesn't work, someday, we'll go through every single tombstone, find each child who is under ten years old, and plant a flower at each. Those will be Trent's friends and our kids."

Since Trent's death, they didn't have to buy birthday presents or Christmas presents or pay for orthodontic appointments or doctors or school clothes. They could spend their money on flowers for the kids' graves. And their son would have a whole group of friends, and none of them would feel left out.

"I would love to do that."

He nodded. "You were always big on nobody feeling left out."

"That's probably because sometimes I felt left out when I was growing up. I had a tendency to be different. My parents were older than everyone else's parents, and I was raised differently for one, and also...I thought orange and pink looked good together for a while."

"In the right setting, they do."

"Only you would agree with me." She paused. "You could build something that would make them look good," she said. Confident that her words were true.

"Because you would design it first."

Again their eyes caught and held. She figured she probably ought to do something before his phone could interrupt him again, so she said, "Ready to see our son's grave?"

"Only if you hold my hand."

She gave him a questioning look, and she realized that maybe he'd never invited her to come because this wasn't a pleasant place for him. That he did not enjoy being here, and maybe he was afraid he would cry. He hadn't shed any tears in their relationship until their son died.

And then, she almost thought he cried harder than she did at the funeral. She had been pretty much cried out, but his tears flowed constantly the entire day.

He cried even harder when the casket had gone into the ground.

Again, she stood, almost stoic.

Maybe that was part of her pulling into herself, and he just couldn't do it.

Not that it was a good thing. It probably wasn't healthy at all, but it was why she had not cried, and he had. And she knew he didn't enjoy it. Didn't necessarily feel manly with tears flowing. Maybe that was why he avoided the cemetery. He held his hand out, and she stared at it over the bed of the pickup.

Then, slowly, she walked around and slipped her hand into his. It was something that they had done a million times but hadn't done for a long while, and it felt familiar and perfect and bright and yet unfamiliar and awkward and odd at the same time.

She wanted it to feel familiar again. She wanted him to be the rock that she leaned on, and she wanted to be the person who supported him through everything, the one he could come home to, the one he could be real with, the one he could go to his son's grave with and cry if he needed to. Knowing that she was there, beside him, and wouldn't ever let go of his hand.

That's what she wanted when she said her marriage vows. She wanted a steadfast love. She wanted forever.

Dominic and Vera walked off the road, and several rows down, to the plot of ground that they had bought at the time Trent had died.

She was probably like every other normal human being and hadn't thought about a burial plot until she needed one.

She was only in her early forties. She wasn't thinking that she was going to need a plot of ground to bury someone at her age.

Her parents had both wanted to be cremated, and that made it easier. Maybe that was why they'd chosen it. To inconvenience her as little as possible.

"This is the first time we've come here together," Dominic said as they reached Trent's grave and stood at the foot of it, looking at the headstone, her eyes caressing the familiar words.

Beloved son.

It had been simple. Nothing out of the ordinary. She hadn't felt like saying anything funny, and of course, Trent had never made his wishes about what he'd like as an epitaph known.

"Sorry about that," Dominic continued. "I should have come here as often as you wanted to."

It was easy to say that. Now that the time was gone. Even at his best, he probably wasn't going to do everything she wanted to every time she wanted to. He was human after all.

But it was easy to say that he should have.

"We should have come together at least once. Maybe last year on his anniversary."

"You came here every day at first."

"I couldn't stand the idea of him being alone. Then, I couldn't stand the idea of me being alone." She didn't know how else to explain it, and maybe there wasn't anything she could explain. It was just feelings. It felt like she needed to be here. This is where she felt comfortable and secure.

"The house felt too...empty. I hated walking around while my footsteps echoed off the walls, and I expected to hear Trent, and I didn't, and I would see a mark on the wall, where he put his grubby hands, and I would think 'I can't wipe it off.' Then I would see the other pristine walls, and wish there were grubby hand marks all over them, and wish so hard that I'd never wiped away any grubby handprints."

She lifted her shoulder. "It was just easier to be here. Even though I knew he wasn't really here."

"Yeah. I knew he wasn't here, and I was like you, I couldn't stand being in the house either. And you know me, I had to be doing something." He paused. "I don't know why I didn't get the material and get started on the plans you had for the backyard and the flowerbeds and everything, except I knew that your plans included a swing set, a sandbox, and a place where he could shoot hoops."

He took a breath, sucking it in and through his teeth. "Just couldn't bring myself to do it."

"I guess both of us had our things that were stumbling blocks. And we handled it in different ways."

"We handled it separately."

His fingers were still threaded with hers, and he tugged a little, so they faced each other at the end of Trent's grave.

"I regret that more than anything. I shouldn't have tried to handle it alone, throwing myself into work, keeping myself busy with projects. That took me away from you. I was the man of the house. I should have been here."

She wasn't quite sure if he was trying to say that he had been with someone else. Was he?

No. She wouldn't let that thought in her head. She was going to ask him at some point, but this was not the time. He was saying all the right things, and she needed to respond to them in all the right ways. It wouldn't help their relationship at all if she responded to his real pain and his apology with guilt and suspicion.

Maybe it was a good time for a subject change.

"This time of year, it feels like I need to be gearing up for T-ball."

He laughed. "Can you believe I actually miss coaching those little guys?"

"He loved that you were the coach. The first year, one of the moms coached their team, and it was okay, but he was just so proud when she couldn't do it the next year, and you said you would."

"I know as much about T-ball as I do about playing the piano, but we had fun."

"The best thing was getting ice cream after every game."

"Yeah. I think I gained about twenty pounds that first spring. Thankfully, T-ball season doesn't last very long."

"I thought you were going to say you were thankful someone else volunteered the next year."

"No. I missed it. That's why I volunteered fast the year after that when that coach couldn't do it anymore."

"I liked it better when you coached. I felt like...like I was more of a part of it or something. I don't know."

"You were married to the man who mattered," he said, winking.

They had turned and were now facing the grave again, their hands still linked between them.

"I had so many things I wanted to do with him. I mean, I would have been fine if he didn't want to be a landscaper. It's a hard job. In the heat in the summer, physical labor, and you gotta hope people want to keep doing things to their land, you know? A downturn in the economy could mean going out of business, but I just... I wanted to share it with him. I couldn't wait for him to... He loved going with me, and maybe he would have outgrown that, but I just couldn't wait for him to be side by side with me, working together, talking about it, making decisions." His voice cracked a little. "I mean, it would have been a family thing, with you and me working together and then bringing our son in. I just can't imagine anything better."

To her surprise, he had started to tear up.

His voice broke on the last word, and he said, "I never really talked about it, because I didn't want him to feel pressure to follow in my footsteps, to do the family business if that wasn't what he wanted."

He wasn't exactly crying, but one tear rolled out of his eye and down his cheek.

Vera had to fight the urge to wrap her arms around him. She hated it when he cried. Not that crying showed weakness exactly, she just hated that he felt broken.

"I didn't know," she said, softly and honestly. Because he was right, he had never said anything about it.

"I know. Like I said, I wanted him to choose, but I loved it on the days that he could go with me. I loved taking him. Yeah, it was more work. Sometimes he got tired, and sometimes I had to tell him he couldn't play on things that he wanted to play on, but... I just had so many hopes that were dashed. Not that I mourn my hopes and dreams more than I mourn my son, I don't. It's just I imagined my future stretching off into eternity and we would never be separated. I was supposed to go first. He was going to take over the company. You and I would retire to a Caribbean island or something."

She snorted over that. "We weren't making that much money."

"You might be surprised how little it costs to live on an island like that, if you're not expecting to have resort standards."

"I want running water and prefer for it to be heated, and I also need an inside toilet that flushes."

"And no bugs."

"Maybe we better stay in Michigan," she said, and for the first time in eighteen months, they laughed together. A true, shared laughter, and it was surprising to her that it was while they were standing at their son's grave.

Of course, he was crying a little, she had a tendency to be more stoic and internalize it, but the fact that they could come here and share memories and some laughter.

"Boy, I don't know, if Trent knew that you and I were expecting him to support us in our retirement on a Caribbean island..."

His smile faded. "Remember when he lost his teeth?"

"He burned his eyebrows off then, too. His face looked really weird."

"Yeah. That's what I was gonna say. It seemed like his whole face felt off or something."

"His first-grade pictures were terrible."

"They're my favorite. It shows what kind of personality he had."

"I suppose it does, although I think we're very blessed that he didn't do more than burn his eyebrows off when he was leaning over the candles..."

"What did he say he was doing again?"

"He was trying to figure out where the fire's roots were or something." She shook her head. She couldn't exactly remember. All she recalled was being absolutely petrified because her son had come into the sunroom missing his eyebrows.

"You know he didn't cry, and he didn't even mention it. I just... looked at him and knew there was something wrong. And finally, I said, 'Trent, where did your eyebrows go?'"

He laughed. "And Trent probably shrugged his shoulders and asked if he could have a cookie or something."

"Actually, I'm pretty sure he asked if he could cook supper."

"He did?"

"Yeah. I think he was trying to get my mind off the fact that his eyebrows were gone. And maybe he didn't want to have to tell me how they disappeared."

"He could have lied about it."

"I know. He always had your steadfast character and integrity. You don't say flippant things, things you don't mean. But more than that, you always tell the truth."

He had gone silent.

A little voice tried to sneak in and say that it was because he felt guilty, but she pushed it aside. This was the first honest conversation they'd had about their son since his death. She was going to enjoy every moment of it.

"Yeah, he didn't lie. I finally prodded him again, and he said, 'I didn't know they were gone.' And then, when I told him they were, and I sniffed the air and said, 'Is something burning?' That's when he said, 'Maybe they burned off. I was looking at the candle.'"

"He was such a character."

"I know. I was scared to death you were going to be mad at me when you got home and your son no longer had eyebrows."

"Why would I be mad at you?"

"Because I wasn't watching him very well."

"But he was six. I mean, he knew he wasn't allowed to play with fire. And from what I understand, he actually wasn't. But still, he was at the age where you didn't expect to have to follow him around with a magnifying glass, checking on everything that he did. You should have been able to sit down and work without your son playing with fire."

"Yeah. That's what I thought too, but I was wrong. It took a little while before I let him out of my sight again."

"I take it he didn't cook supper."

"No. He did not."

"I can just imagine all the trouble he's getting into up in heaven."

"He'd be ten. He was eight and a half when he passed. Can you imagine him older?"

"I always thought we'd have a pile of kids."

"Me too. I was an only child, and I really wanted more..." Her voice trailed off. She didn't want to make him feel guilty, as she didn't want to rehash the past. "I'm a little too old now. But we have our kids, this group of cemetery children. Although we're going to have to think of something else to call them."

"The Raspberry Ridge Children's Fun Club," Dominic said, in an announcer type of voice.

"Well. That's quite a mouthful, and hopefully we'll never have to write invitations with that on it."

"No. I guess we can count our blessings."

"We have so many, don't we?" She looked over at him, not really wanting to be serious, wanting to keep the conversation light. After all, they could have more conversations, if this one went well. But she didn't want to derail it and ruin the tremulous bond that had been growing between them. It needed to be a little stronger before she could test it with anything weighty.

"We sure do. I think sometimes it's hard to remember, because we get lost in all of the bad things, but think about the memories we have. Some people don't even have those."

"You're right. Some people don't." And she thought that maybe he didn't. He had had a rough childhood and had determined that his child would not have the same, but he didn't talk about it a whole lot, other than he wanted something different for his kid.

"I'm glad we came today. I enjoyed reminiscing. I thought it would be more painful, but it actually felt...healing."

"Yeah. For me too. I've avoided the graveyard because I thought it would be a sad place. A painful place, like you. But I actually had fun." He grunted a laugh that was half disbelief. "I have a whole bunch more memories that are just swimming at the top of my head, things I hadn't thought about for a really long time, but things that are happy to look back on. There was just one sad time. Other than that, I can't think of a thing, other than occasionally losing a ball game."

"We got ice cream even if we lost, so losing wasn't really that bad, at least in my opinion."

"I don't think the kids cared, either. Although, maybe if we didn't get ice cream if they lost, it would have inspired them to play a little harder."

"They were just little kids. They didn't need to play hard. I love that you kept it fun for them."

"I guess there's no reason why I couldn't still volunteer."

"It seemed like they were scrambling for a coach every single year. They probably still are, and they'd love to have you volunteer."

"I wouldn't do it unless you were my co-coach."

"Me? I don't know anything about T-ball."

"That equals the number of things that I knew about it when I started. And if they took me, they'll take you too."

"I think you can probably fake it a little better than I can. I don't look like a T-ball coach."

"Are you saying I do?"

"You were a pretty handsome T-ball coach, back in the day."

"Back in the day?" He pretended to be offended. "It wasn't that long ago."

"Well, you have a little more gray in your hair than you used to. Of course, so do I." She looked away. If she weren't so old, maybe they could try for another child. Two children. She would love to do that, but she felt like she was a little late getting started. And after having Trent, she didn't want to go through the heartbreak of hope, and then failure, and depression.

"Let's go back and get the flowers, and then, if we have time, we could write down every name of every child under ten and get started with our Raspberry Ridge Children's Fun Club."

"All right. I like that idea."

Nineteen

Dominic and Vera went back, and it didn't take long to plant flowers at the five graves, and then they went through the cemetery, which wasn't overly large, and found eight more graves of kids who had passed away at less than ten years of age, making a total of thirteen including Trent.

He loved how Vera's eyes shone as she wrote down notes for each one. She even wrote down where they could find them again so they didn't have to hunt too hard.

Vera was good at keeping track of things like that. He was much more likely to come back and hunt them up every time or rely on his memory.

He had forgotten how much he enjoyed being with her, doing things with her, working with her.

"I think that's enough to make a softball team."

"They could have a basketball team too, only five players on the floor at a time, but there have to be some substitutes, which you need throughout the game."

"How many people on a hockey team? They can play that in the winter."

"Five on the ice at a time, I think, but don't forget it does not have to be about sports."

"We could have an orchestra right here."

"That we could. We can assign each one of them an instrument, and make them practice for the next twenty years, and we might have something that sounds halfway decent."

"What exactly are you trying to say?"

"That you took lessons the exact right amount of time," he said, pretending to be scared that she was going to be upset with him.

He enjoyed sitting in the music room and listening to her play. In fact, when they had purchased their house, that was one of the things he had insisted on, that they have a music room. Because it was something she loved.

Come to think of it, he hadn't heard her play since the funeral either.

Maybe today's visit would be cathartic in that way.

He almost said something, but then figured he wouldn't. There would be time another day to push her to pick up her instrument again.

"That was the right answer, I'd say," she said, giving him a wry smile, as they looked at the last grave.

"I would like to go and buy eight more flowers, so they have them for this year."

"Yeah. I was thinking the same thing. I don't want them to feel left out."

"That whole feeling left out thing again."

"I'm sensitive." She shrugged, like it couldn't be helped.

"I know. Sometimes people have to go through hard things so that they can be stronger, but sometimes it's nice to just not have to do the hard things, and...correct me if I'm wrong, but it kind of feels like these kids have already done the hard thing."

"That's true. It's not like we can spoil them."

"Exactly."

He turned around, and so did she, standing right beside him.

It was more of a natural thing than anything, that his hand came up and he put it around her.

But after he did, it felt right. As they looked out over the graveyard, the flowers that they had brought brightening up the entire place and the idea that there would be eight more flowers for eight more children soon made him smile as well.

"Thanks for coming with me today."

"Thanks for suggesting it. I think it was well past time."

"Yeah. I should have suggested it a long time ago."

"But we can only start from here and move forward."

He looked over at her and narrowed his eyes a bit. It almost sounded like...like she was ready to move on.

He was too. He had been for a while.

Their foray into the graveyard had not fixed everything, but it had made Vera completely forget about checking the scheduling site on the computer.

When they got home, she had gone outside and worked in the flowerbeds for a while. She didn't want the weeds to get ahead of her, and after that, she had showered and dropped into bed before she remembered.

She shoved the thought out of her head, because she didn't want it to keep her from falling asleep. And she didn't want to ruin the day.

She felt closer to her husband, like the gulf that was between them wasn't impassable anymore.

It was funny how a little bit of conversation, a little bit of laughter, even a tear or two, could bond people together.

She and Dominic didn't have to have every single thing in common for them to know that they were perfect for each other.

She was confident that they would figure out what was wrong and work things out.

But in the morning, she had to go and visit Miles and Norma Jean. She had promised Mrs. Calvin that she would do that, and she wanted to keep her promise. She also was feeling a little more optimistic about her own marriage, like she might be able to help another couple with theirs. On that thought, she rolled over and went right to sleep.

Twenty-One

Norma Jean stood at the stove, discouraged.

She and Miles had agreed to a marriage of convenience, and she had agreed to go live with him, helping him with his daughter, Holly, and doing what he needed done, in exchange for him providing a home for her.

She thought that having the home, when she hadn't really had a very good one before, would be enough. It seemed romantic at the time, but now...it seemed like a foolish mistake, since Miles barely gave her the time of day and slept on the couch.

He didn't even really care whether she had made supper or done anything other than take rudimentary care of Holly.

She thought she was so smart and clever and funny, but it turned out that she wasn't any of that.

Not to mention, she had dreams of having a big garden, and going into Raspberry Ridge and selling produce and helping earn money for the farm, but she hadn't realized she had a black thumb, and everything that she tried to grow failed.

A knock at the door made her look up from the soup she stirred at the stove.

A peek at her bread showed that it wasn't rising, and she must have done something wrong.

Fiddlesticks. And then she laughed at herself. Nobody said fiddlesticks anymore, but she had Holly, so she couldn't say the words that she might have been used to saying.

"I'm coming," she called. Then she stopped. "The door's unlocked. You can come in." Holly was at school, and even if she wasn't, she wouldn't knock before she came in, so she knew it wasn't her.

The door opened, and a woman she had never seen before stepped in.

She had just gotten married and moved to Raspberry Ridge, so it made sense that she didn't know too many people, but she didn't even know whether this one was local or not. She might be selling something.

Drying her hands on a dish towel, she set it on the table and came over. "I'm Norma Jean Everhart." She got a little thrill when she mentioned her married name. That definitely was not real yet. "It's nice to meet you."

"I am Vera Miller, and it's nice to meet you. I live on the hill, on the other end of Raspberry Ridge."

"You're a neighbor," Norma Jean said, and she couldn't keep the excitement out of her voice. She'd been feeling very alone and was so happy to have another woman to talk to.

"I'm sorry I didn't realize you moved in. I heard from the former pastor's wife, Mrs. Calvin," Vera said.

"Bless her heart. She was a sweetheart. She and her husband seem to keep tabs on what goes on here, despite retiring. My husband has mentioned them. His family was fond of them and went to the church until it closed."

"I'd like to see the church reopen, but so far, no one seems interested, and I'm not even sure we're looking anymore."

"That's too bad. It's a nice building. If it just sits there with nothing happening to it, it'll fall into disrepair."

"Yes. Buildings take maintenance, and so do people, and so do relationships."

Norma Jean bit her lip and looked away. She didn't know how to do maintenance on her relationship. She didn't even know how to get started on her relationship. She barely knew Miles, and...

"Are you okay?" Vera said, coming over closer and putting a hand on Norma Jean's shoulder.

"I am. Mostly. Do you have time to sit and chat for a bit?"

"I sure do. That's what I was hoping to do when I came."

"Well, let me grab some sweet tea out of the fridge. Is that okay?"

"Whatever you have is fine."

"I might have had homemade bread, but... I keep doing something wrong, and my bread doesn't rise." She sighed, and then the rest of the story came out. "Miles's sister-in-law is proficient in everything, perfect, and never does a thing wrong. I'm a little jealous and very intimidated. I can't do anything as good as she can."

"That makes you feel inferior, doesn't it?"

She nodded, thankful the tears that pricked her eyes did not fall. "Miles never really says anything, he just says, 'Laura can do this' and 'Laura can do that,' and that's not what I can do," Norma Jean said, sighing again as she set the tea on the table and then went back to the cupboard for glasses.

"What *can* you do?" Vera asked gently.

"I don't know. That's a good question. I feel like I can't do anything right now."

"Well, there are two things you can do, you can either learn to do the things that your husband wants you to do, which I kinda suggest you should do, or you should double down on the things you're good at and be the very best that you can be with those things. And then just admit that nobody can be the best at everything."

"I guess I want to do both of those things."

Vera laughed. "Well, that's not impossible. But it's going to take some determination." Vera narrowed her eyes. "You look like a very determined woman."

"I used to think I was. I set my eye on what I want, and then I go after it, but...it's kind of hard to do that when you just feel broken down all the time. Or like you just don't measure up."

"There's a reason your husband fell in love with you," Vera said with confidence and a sweet smile that made Norma Jean feel uncomfortable.

"Actually, we didn't fall in love."

"Okay..." Vera said slowly, like she was treading on unfamiliar ground and wasn't sure whether she would be stepping on a land mine. "Do you want to talk about that?" Vera said, again slowly.

Norma Jean fiddled with her glass. "I guess there's not a whole lot to talk about. We ended up in a marriage of convenience. I am pretty much pathetic at everything. He's a farmer, and I'm a pathetic farmer's wife. He knew me well enough to know that before we got married, and I'm not sure why he's with me now. Why he agreed to a marriage of convenience."

"Why did you?"

"I guess I thought I would have a family. You know, something I never had before."

"That's hard. And sad. I'm sorry."

"It's okay. I turned out okay, or maybe that's arrogant. I don't mean it in an arrogant way. I just... I don't think I was terrible. I just wanted people around me who loved me unconditionally. You know? Someone to be there whenever you screw up." She looked over at the counter. "Someone to commiserate when your bread doesn't rise."

"Someone to tell you what you did wrong when your bread doesn't rise," Vera said with a laugh. "I guess I'm not like normal women who want to just sit around and cry over their failures. I want to figure out what the problem was and fix it."

"That's probably a better, and more constructive, attitude."

"I've made a few loaves of bread in my time, although it's been a few years. One of the things that can make that happen is that the water you dissolve the yeast in is too hot. Or your yeast might be too old."

"I don't know how old the yeast is. I found it in the cupboard."

"There's a way to prove that," Vera said, standing.

"There is?"

"Yeah. Come on over here, and I'll show you. It involves a little bit of yeast, sugar, and some water."

"All right."

Norma Jean went over and watched while Vera explained what she was doing, doing it a little bit slowly, which Norma Jean really appreciated.

"Now," Vera said as she mixed it in a small bowl. "We can go over there to the table and sit down and talk, and give this a few minutes. If the yeast is good, it will start bubbling and foaming, the more bubbling and foaming we have, the better the yeast is. If nothing happens, then we found the problem."

"That sounds amazing. How did you know that?" Norma Jean said.

"I probably found it online. I experimented with making bread for a while when I was pregnant with my son. I had all these cravings for yeasty bread that were just crazy over-the-top. And so I started making bread. I was terrible at it at first, but I kept working on it, and while I wouldn't say that I actually got good, I got where I could make a loaf of bread that was edible, and actually, if you put enough butter on it, it was excellent, I would say."

"So are you a chef?" Norma Jean asked and then realized it was a dumb question. She had to teach herself to make bread. She obviously wasn't a chef.

"No. I'm a designer. I design gardens and work with plants and the containers that house them, paths, patios, and waterfalls mostly. Sometimes retaining walls and that type of thing. And my husband..." Her voice trailed off for a moment, and then she said, "My husband builds the things. Whatever I design. He's a genius at putting things together and taking things from a piece of paper and making something concrete and absolutely stunning out of it."

"You guys have the kind of relationship that I hoped I would have. Where the two of you are a team. Working together, complementing each other."

She couldn't help it, her voice was a little sad as she traced a finger over the condensation that had gathered on her glass.

"It's kind of like we said before, relationships are a work in progress. They take tending. And... I don't even know how to start when you started with something so crazy like a marriage of convenience."

"I know. I probably shouldn't have jumped into it, but it seemed like a good idea to do at the time."

"Sometimes something that you think is your biggest mistake turns out to be the best thing you ever did. You know, that might be this."

"Do you think?" Norma Jean asked, hope maybe not blossoming in her chest, but it kind of peeked through the soil a little bit. Maybe looking around, seeing if it might want to grow some.

"I know. I'm sure of it. The Bible commands us to love people, so I know it's quite possible to decide that you're going to love someone, even if you don't know them. And the Bible also commands us to love our husbands, so do you think God would command us to do something that we weren't able to do?"

"Even if we got married in a marriage of convenience?"

"I'm pretty sure all the marriages back then were marriages of convenience, and yet God commanded wives to love their husbands, and he commanded husbands to love their wives. So, God must have decided that even if you didn't fall in love, and there's nothing about falling in love in the Bible, there was a way for you to love that person."

"I've never considered that. I guess I just thought falling in love was the right thing to do. You know, find the right person, fall in love."

"But you didn't fall in love with your husband?"

"Well, I kind of had a crush on another guy, and I didn't get married out of spite exactly, but I guess he was in the right place at the right time."

"However it happened, you can make something beautiful out of it. I mean, through the Lord, anything is possible, right?"

"Yes. I believe that. But I never thought to apply that to my marriage. I would really love to have a strong marriage where we work together and...where he loves me." Her voice lowered, and she looked down at the table. She knew it was probably a pipe dream. She had done so many terrible things, how in the world could Miles ever decide he was going to love her? He'd seen her at her worst.

"I guess the first thing you have to do is believe that it's possible. And then after that, it's just a matter of working toward your goal."

"But how?"

"I think the Bible gives us an answer again. If you become the kind of woman the Bible wants you to be, I would guess that a man can't help but be attracted to that. The right kind of man, anyway." Vera paused. "I assume your husband is a Christian?"

"Yeah."

"A true Christian man who loves Jesus will be attracted to a woman who is living what the Bible teaches."

"How do I find out what the Bible teaches about what a woman is supposed to be?"

"Proverbs 31 is a great place to start. Titus 2 has some wisdom in it too."

"Do you really think that would work?"

"I don't know. Men are a little more complicated than women are."

"Boy, you can say that again."

They laughed together, and then Vera said, "I can tell you this much, I'll pray for you. That'll give you an edge, for starters. And then, if you want, we can meet weekly and discuss the Bible passages I mentioned or anything you want. Becoming a woman who is beautiful in God's eyes will make you beautiful in your husband's eyes."

"Oh. Well, I never even thought about that."

"The Bible has all the instructions we need, and...not that I think that you need to change, not for your husband, but for the Lord. That's probably the right reason, although we can have ulterior motives, can't we?" Vera said, and her smile was so engaging, so cute and fun, that Norma Jean found herself smiling along and meaning it. It was the first real smile she felt in days.

Twenty-Two

"I was going to go plant the rest of the flowers on the graves today, and then I was going to get started working on the healing garden." Dominic paused for a moment, his eyes on the sky, the brilliant sunrays seeming to stretch from the eastern side to the western side, with it becoming all that more brilliant from the reflection on Lake Michigan.

He took a breath. "I was hoping you'd go and help me today."

He said the words softly, humbly. He was asking her, letting her know that she was what he wanted.

She hesitated a couple of beats longer than she might have back a few years ago. *Before...* But her answer made him smile.

"Sure. I was planning on doing the same things, and I'd love to do them with you."

"You must have noticed that I got the dozer work done, and it's gone."

"I saw that yesterday when I came home from visiting Norma Jean."

"It's always fun to get to play in one of those things, but it's even more fun to get a design started, to know that it's in my hands. I'm really excited about it. All the material should be down there right now. It was supposed to be delivered yesterday evening. I have the bill of ladings, and I'm going to check and make sure we got everything."

"All right. I can take a few containers of water and make sure all the plants survived okay."

"I figured you would." It's what she always did. He got the tools and supplies, she always dealt with the live plants.

"I ordered a bunch of topsoil too. I'm pretty sure I saw a pile there yesterday, but it was back off the road, probably so no one would steal it, and I didn't go over and check."

"Did we hear back from the township about electricity?" she asked.

"Not yet. I had half a mind to ask Homer what he thought about supplying electricity from his garage. It's not that far, and it would save us a lot of red tape with the township. They might decline us because of the fountain, because of not knowing who was going to pay for it. Even if I made a donation that would cover the electricity for the next fifty years, I can still see someone having an issue. Of course, that would mean that Homer was responsible for the electricity, and he might not want that responsibility."

"I bet he'll take it. I think he'll be on board. Didn't you talk to him about it a little bit?"

"I did, and he seemed really interested, but...it's one thing to be interested, it's another thing to donate the money to pay for something."

"Maybe we could put a little donation box up, and he could be in charge of getting the money from it, and if there was anything extra, he could either hire someone to take care of it, or... I don't know."

"That's actually not a bad idea, although, again, it might be more responsibility than what he wants to face. I don't know how busy he is with his job and the other things he has to do."

"We won't know until we ask," she said.

They fell into silence, which was just fine by him. Typically in the morning, they didn't talk a whole lot. But their conversation felt less forced. More natural. Less like he was walking through a minefield. There were a few times not that long ago where he wasn't sure that he might not ruin everything by saying the wrong thing.

He wasn't sure why he thought that. Vera had never been a hard person to talk to, and she never took offense easily.

His phone rang, and he saw it was Shoshana. He'd let her calls go to voicemail twice the day they visited the cemetery, because he didn't want to interrupt his time with Vera, but he had forgotten to call her the rest of the day or even yesterday. He'd been kind of wrapped up in his memories. It was the first time that he really allowed himself to think about his son and remember the good times. The good far outweighed the bad, and in this life, he knew that no one was promised tomorrow. He was glad that they had made so many good memories, so many fun times, so many things he cherished.

There weren't too many bad times. And like he had told his wife, for that he was grateful.

But he supposed he needed to deal with Shoshana now.

"I'm gonna take this inside," he said, and opening the door, he walked into the house. He didn't want to ruin Vera's sunrise just because he had to deal with Shoshana.

"Hello?" he said. He wasn't quite sure why she was getting up so early, because when he worked with her before, it had been hard at times for them to touch base because she was starting her day about the time he was ending his.

"Dominic. If I didn't know better, I would think you were avoiding me."

"Well, you know better, so there's that."

He was avoiding her. But he didn't want to say that. Reminding himself that he wanted to stay on good terms with her, just in case there was going to be any benefit to Vera, he tried to shake off the annoyance that she didn't seem to be able to take no for an answer, and she wouldn't stop bothering him.

Her laughter trilled, and then she said, "Oh, you are a funny one."

He wondered if maybe she hadn't gone to bed yet. She sounded too chipper for this hour in the morning for someone who wasn't typically a morning person.

"So, what do I have to do to talk you into taking this project with me? Now, I can hear you right now, saying that you're too busy. But you do realize the benefits to both of us when we do this, correct?"

"I know there are benefits to working in Hollywood. There are a lot of people who would notice."

"And it would solidify you and me as the top design landscaping team in the United States. You're already sought after, imagine what this will do to your career. You'll be able to hire enough people to keep up with all the jobs that you'll be getting. You could have a team in every state. Just think about how this is going to look for you. You won't ever have to worry about money again, that's for sure. You can command the price that you want on every job that you do. I guarantee it."

He wondered if she would back that guarantee with a little bit of cold hard cash. Something told him she wouldn't.

It was interesting to him how she was pitching it being about all the benefits he was going to have. Like she wasn't getting any. He almost snorted at the thought. It was going to benefit her far more than him. She was the one who wanted the job, and she was the one who couldn't get it without him.

So she was buttering him up.

"Dominic? Hello? I didn't get you out of bed, did I?"

"No. I was up."

"I figured you would be. You're such an early riser. So rustic."

"Yeah."

"All right. So I'm in California now, do me a favor and just come out and look at it. I'll take you out for dinner, we'll do a fancy restaurant, have you heard of Richard's?"

"No."

"Well, it's booked solid two weeks out, but I can get us a table. You name your day, and you and me, we'll make a day of it. After all, I miss working with you."

They never even met. They had done all their work together online. They spent a good bit of time on the phone, but it had been one project, one time. Five phone calls, tops. No more than an hour each. If that.

How could she miss him?

It wasn't like they talked every day or something.

"I'll think about it," he finally said. Maybe he could talk to Vera, see if she thought there would be any benefit to him keeping Shoshana on a string. He hated to put it that way, but it kind of felt like what he was doing, since he wasn't interested in going to California to work. He cut back on everything, except a job he was doing for a municipality just two hours north of Raspberry Ridge. Beyond that and beyond finishing the job his guys were currently working on, he didn't know where he was going from there.

He hated to lay his guys off, but he knew people who knew people and might be able to get them onto a good crew. They were good guys. He only worked with the best, when he could get them.

Except, he had lowered his standards for Shoshana. She might have the fancy awards and accolades, but in his mind, his wife was hands down better. All the way around.

"How long is it going to take, you think? We need to let them know in two weeks."

She sounded like she was pouting a little, but she didn't sound irritated. Maybe she was being as careful with him as he was with her, maybe she saw the benefits of working with him. Maybe she was trying to get the benefits of being known as the designer who worked with Vera's husband.

After all, Vera wasn't exactly nationally known, but she definitely was well loved in certain circles, and her work was always given the highest ratings.

He laughed to himself. Maybe he'd been looking at it all wrong. Maybe it was Shoshana who was getting all of the benefits.

Now *that* made sense.

And here he thought he was helping his wife.

"I'll let you know within two weeks," he finally said, wanting to tell her no and be done with it.

He had walked through the house and stood staring out the window at the driveway, at the flower boxes that he'd just made for his wife. He didn't need to work, and neither did she. Although he thought both of them would be happier if they did, but they could afford to be choosy and only do the projects that had the two of them working together.

Right there, standing there looking at the flower boxes as Shoshana hung up the phone, he vowed to himself that he would never work with anyone but his wife again. It just wasn't worth it.

Twenty-Three

Vera smiled as she came out of the house; her husband was waiting on her.

It was eight o'clock, exactly when the garden center opened. They should get there before the crowds.

She had thought about going in and checking her computer, but she caught up on some laundry and did a little bit of housework, even though it didn't feel like the house had gotten dirty. She still swept all the carpets, swept and scrubbed the hardwood and tile flooring, and dusted everything in sight.

She was still thinking about that design, and sometimes doing housework, keeping her hands busy while her mind was free to create, helped burst through the block in her head.

But not today.

"You ready?" her husband said as she came down the stairs.

He was dusty, sawdust stuck to his pants and shirt. It looked like he had brushed some of it off but missed a little. Typical of Dominic. He wasn't nearly the neat freak she was. Although, he was very particular when it came to measurements.

And building.

"I am. It looks like you've been doing something in the shop."

He was quiet for a minute, nodding his head and looking down, before he said, "Yeah. I just had in my head I wanted to make some crosses for those kids. I mean obviously they all have gravestones, so they don't need a cross from me, but I was putting them together and burning their names in them."

It was a technique that she liked. He would use the router to router their names in an italic or fancy font, and then he would use the torch to burn the wood where the name was. Then he might put a finish on the wood. It ended up that the name was a darker black, with wood grain, while the wood was a lighter brown.

It would look really neat on their crosses.

"Would you show me?" she asked.

He had already started to come to the steps to meet her and had his hand out, like he was going to put it around her.

"Sure." He shrugged a shoulder. "I... I really didn't have any specific idea for what to do with them..." His voice trailed off, like he was a little embarrassed.

She understood; her heart had been touched by the children in the graveyard as well. Thirteen kids. Thirteen sets of parents who had been just as devastated as she and Dominic. Thirteen families who lost someone's smiles and laughter and fun and energy and whose houses were a little quieter, who had beds that were empty, teddy bears that weren't being squeezed anymore, ice cream that wasn't eaten, and T-ball games that missed one little person.

She thought particularly of the mothers. Some of them probably had other children and had to continue on, living their lives, and didn't have the luxury that she had, enough money and no other little bodies who needed her attention, so she could afford to stay in bed all day if she wanted to. And she had at times. She could afford to get up and go to the cemetery and sit there all day, and she had. What would it have been like to have been forced to go on, even when she didn't feel like she could?

She wasn't sure, but regardless of their different circumstances, she didn't know what they were, but she did know a mother's heart. And how it felt when it was broken. How it felt when it healed, not quite whole, because there was a piece missing.

She loved that Dominic had obviously been thinking about them too. Only, he used action to think. He had to be using his hands, building and creating something, and so he made crosses.

She followed him into the shop, and there they were, thirteen of them lined up, the paper that she'd scribbled down the names and dates and locations of them lying on the workbench. He'd obviously used it to get the names so he could router them in.

They weren't huge, maybe eighteen inches high and six or so inches for the crossbeam.

"They're beautiful. They...deserve a setting."

"I kinda thought you might think that. But I didn't want you to feel pressure. I just... I needed to do something, you know?"

"I know. That's how you handle things, you do something, use your hands, get active. And I do the opposite. I turn inward and contemplate things, thinking about them until they make sense to me, and I feel like I can come out again and join the world."

"I'm glad you were able to come out and join the world. I missed you."

Their eyes met, and she felt the slow twirling of her stomach.

She almost put a hand over it. But this was her husband. She'd been married to him for more than a decade. It wasn't like he was unfamiliar to her, but maybe unfamiliar in the sense that it had been a year and a half since she had looked at him and felt anything but sadness, and perhaps anger or jealousy.

But now she looked at him, a man, hurt by the death of his son, and not knowing how to handle it. Maybe he could have done better, but maybe, she could have too.

And now, his heart was touched by thirteen children, twelve of whom he didn't even know.

"Can I use them in the healing garden?" she asked, sudden inspiration going on in her brain. She wanted to go open her laptop and create. But she'd promised to spend the day with her husband. But what she was thinking was something that could evolve over the day, and she could take notes on it so she wouldn't forget.

"Of course." He looked surprised. "Don't feel like you have to. I wasn't really thinking anything specific."

"I wasn't thinking that I had to, but I just had an idea for a design that would be perfect. I told you I was struggling, and this is just absolutely the best. I obviously will need to work on it some, but I definitely will use these, if you let me."

"Of course." He looked pleased.

They smiled at each other, and while she noticed that his smile seemed genuine and almost like...like it had looked before they had gotten married, part of her mind was whirling with thoughts of the design that she wanted.

But even though she wanted to whip out her phone and take some notes on it, she figured they could at least walk to the truck together, and she walked to him, slipping her hand into his.

She smiled up at him, looking to see his reaction, still a little unsure.

His brows raised, and then his smile broadened.

"Now I'm ready to go," she said.

They drove to the garden center and got eight more geraniums.

It didn't take long to plant them at the graveyard, although they probably lingered longer than they needed to, as they looked at the gravestones. One child had been born and died in the 1980s. And they had remarked that it would have been so odd to have only lived in one decade. She didn't feel super old, but she'd lived in five different decades. Although, the one she'd been born in she didn't know too much about, because it had been over before she knew what a decade was.

Still, to be born in the 80s and to die in the 80s. It made her sad.

"I wonder where their parents are?" she asked.

"Raspberry Ridge used to be a bigger town back when we were kids, remember?"

"I know. It's kinda sad the way people move away, and apartments aren't rented, houses are abandoned or even torn down. There's actually a mansion on the hill that's empty."

"I know. The Jardine mansion seems so lonely. And there's another, although I think that that one is being taken care of by a skeleton crew, or maybe a temporary crew comes in once every few months or something. I've seen people there."

"Oh. I guess I just haven't paid attention. But I suppose you could be right."

"I haven't seen much happening with the Jardine family. Their girls were behind us in school, but I remember them. They were kinda cute. Little pigtails, and their height in stairsteps. I think there was exactly eighteen months between them or something."

"I don't remember a lot about them."

"I mowed their yard. That was the first lawn care job I ever had. I started when I was ten. It was a lot of grass, and sometimes I thought I'd never get it done, but I got paid pretty well, and it definitely started my career. I probably owe them, but I never really thought about it."

"Well, maybe they'll move back. I don't know why they left to begin with."

"Maybe they haven't. Maybe there's still someone in there. I'm not sure."

Vera never saw any cars in the driveway, but it was set back up off the road, a little higher on the bluff, overlooking the lake. It had an unobstructed view of the lake that must have been pretty spectacular.

They finished planting the flowers, and then, before they left, they went over and looked at their son's grave again.

Neither one of them said they wanted to, it was just something they did, without talking about it.

They stood like they had yesterday, standing together, holding hands, looking at the headstone.

Quiet. Lost in their own thoughts.

"Have you ever thought about trying for another one?" Dominic's voice came out of nowhere, and his question hit her hard.

"No. I'm too old." Her words were short, curt, and final.

She turned and started walking away, but his hand held firm, and he tugged gently. She stopped, her back to him.

"Sorry. I didn't say that to upset you. I said it because there were a lot of times, both before Trent passed away and after, that I thought about adopting. I always wanted a big family, and I thought you did too, and while I loved the family that we had, I've thought about kids that don't have a family and wondered if maybe we could share a little of what we have. It seems too good to keep to ourselves."

Her eyes filled with tears, and she couldn't turn back to face him.

She didn't know why she was tempted to cry, but she tried not to let them spill out.

She wanted another child, almost as much as she wanted her next breath, but she couldn't face the disappointment of month after month of knowing that there would be no child that month. And again, and again. How long? Until menopause hit?

And then, it would be final, and she would be even more devastated. And she'd heard so many stories of adoptions not working out. Of parents getting their hopes up, only to be dashed at the last minute.

"I don't think I can take the devastation," she said, closing her eyes, knowing it was a selfish statement, even as it came out of her mouth. "Losing Trent was more than I could bear. It felt like it was a cross too heavy." She let out her breath. "I made it through, I know. But... Please don't ask me to do that again."

"Don't ask you to love again?" he asked softly.

"Don't ask me to lose what I love again."

Maybe that was part of her hesitation for reconciling with her husband. After all, the deeper and harder a person loved, the more devastating and terrible it was when a person lost the one they loved.

"We'll do what you want," her husband said softly. He didn't point out how selfish she was being, didn't point out how foolish it was to think the way she was thinking. Even though she knew it. She knew that it was better to love deeply and fully and to lose, even if that meant pain and suffering and heartbreak, than it was to never love at all.

And they had plenty. They could adopt four children easily, five, six. That might be a little overboard.

But two. They could be the quintessential American family with 2.5 children, and... She laughed. It made her tears fall out, but she used the back of her wrist to wipe them off.

"You're sounding a little crazy right now."

"Sorry. I really am sorry, but I just thought, we could adopt two children and we would be the quintessential American family, with 2.5 children."

He laughed. "Trent would be the .5."

"Exactly." They laughed together.

Maybe it wasn't funny, maybe the humor was inappropriate, but it just struck them both as funny, and she could almost feel herself healing as the laughter seeped through her soul.

"I think the .5 would need to come first. So it would be .5 plus 2," Dominic finally said, pulling her a little closer to him, although just holding her hand, he didn't put his arm around her.

"Yeah. And in that regard, we wouldn't be the quintessential American family, because we'd still be a little bit odd."

"I like being odd."

They grinned at each other and then turned without saying anything more and walked to the truck.

How did one combat a loss?

The answer came to her on the walk back. It was love and laughter that would heal.

Maybe, maybe a person wasn't ready for love and laughter immediately following a huge loss, but that was what would heal the soul and make them whole again. And maybe, maybe Dominic was right. Maybe that would involve adopting children. Although, maybe that's what they were doing with the graveyard kids, adopting children who didn't have anyone to put flowers on their grave, but it seemed like a small thing, putting flowers on a grave once a year versus adopting children. That was a big responsibility, and she wasn't as young as she used to be.

She tucked that idea away for later.

Twenty-Four

Dominic stood up from the pile of boards he was looking at. Everything was there. He took the papers that he had stapled together, flipped them back so they were right where they belonged, then rolled them up and shoved them in his back pocket.

He was ready to get started, anytime. But he was getting a little hungry, and he thought he would see if Vera was interested in going to get something to eat before they got into the hard work.

He straightened and looked around for his wife, finding her back where she had been sitting for the last hour or so while he was checking the boards. She had done the same with the plants, watered them and then taken a seat with her phone out, sitting cross-legged on the ground, punching things into her phone.

He'd seen her like that before, and he knew she was thinking about the design. Probably making notes of all the things that she wanted to do tonight when she got home and could get to her computer to work.

He would try not to keep her out too late, but he supposed she could stay home tomorrow, and he could work on this himself. He was going to need to take a few things down anyway, a couple of his saws and his generator for starters

As he looked around, he noticed that a man had come out of the creamy yellow house at the edge of the road and started walking toward them.

Dominic recognized Homer.

"It feels warm today. I think winter has finally left us," he said as he held his hand out for Homer.

The other man grinned and shook it. "Sometimes it hangs on with gripping fingers, especially here in Michigan."

To Dominic's knowledge, Homer had never lived anywhere else.

"So how's it going? I mean, obviously nothing's been built yet, but it looks like a lot of supplies have arrived."

"They have. I think everything we need is here, other than a few extras like my saws and generator and that type of thing."

"If you need electricity, you're welcome to plug into the outlet in my garage. I've got my lawnmower in there, and Mom has a few tubs and stuff stored in there, but you can get to the outlets, although I have to admit the overhead light is burnt out. I haven't replaced it, but I can."

"Well, that would be the least I could do for using your electricity. Although, are you sure? It's probably going to take a good bit."

"Not a big deal. I'm excited about what you're building. It's going to improve our view. In fact, you already have getting rid of the scrub brush and everything."

"I was just talking to my wife," Vera appeared at his side, "Speaking of, you remember Vera."

"I sure do," Homer said, holding his hand out to Vera.

As he did, Dominic realized that perhaps Homer had given up the opportunity to be married because he had decided to stay with his mom after his dad left her.

Dominic knew that a lot of people might think that was sad, but he really admired Homer for that, the sacrifice that Homer had made in order that his mom wouldn't be alone.

There weren't exactly a lot of single, eligible women available in Raspberry Ridge, and if Homer was going to be taking care of Gertie as she succumbed to Alzheimer's, it wasn't like he was going to be going anywhere to meet anyone.

Dominic admired the sacrifice.

"Anyway, I was saying, I was talking to my wife about the electricity that we're going to need to run the fountain."

"Do you need a power outlet, or do you need an actual electrical box?"

"We probably need a box, but an outlet would work. We...have applied to the township, but we're betting that the township is going to turn it down. Even if I were to make a donation that would cover fifty years of electrical usage, someone would have to plug it in, turn it on, and turn it off in the winter, obviously it wouldn't run when it's below freezing. Someone would have to make sure maintenance was performed on it, which I would do as long as I'm alive. But we just figured that we might have to change the design to not have a water fountain."

"What if I donated the electricity?" Homer said, and Dominic looked at Vera, both of them grinning.

"We were going to ask you about that. I was just trying to figure out how."

"Are you serious?" Homer said, laughing a little. "Because I'm excited about the idea of the water fountain, and I know that it will be a nice place for my mom. She used to have a huge garden, right there." He pointed to what mostly looked like a weed patch.

"I remember. She grew so much produce, she could give vegetables to everyone in town. She had blueberries and raspberries and strawberries, and she had a couple dwarf fruit trees. She just could make anything grow, and it always looked amazing."

Homer nodded his head. "She loved taking care of it, and after Dad left, she kind of threw herself into it for a few years, but the last couple years as her memory has been slipping, she hasn't worked as hard at it. She does more sitting, the kind of contemplation that I imagine people would do in your healing garden."

"Yeah. Probably."

"And I think a waterfall or fountain or some kind of water sound would be very soothing for her. I... I would be happy to donate the electricity for that. I'll do it, and who knows if the township might pick it up someday."

"Maybe I'll have to run for township supervisor," Dominic joked, but he should have known Vera wouldn't think that was funny.

"You're right. It's a great idea. I'm going to look into what it takes for you to get on the ballot next election cycle."

He shook his head. He should have kept his mouth shut. But Vera was probably right, he should do it. Someone should be on there, and he bet that it was probably hard to find people who wanted to put the time in.

"So, back to the water fountain, I can't tell you how much usage it would be every month. We can set up a solar-powered pump, but it will probably still add something to your regular electric bill."

"Oh. I never even thought about a solar pump. And you know what, they'll probably improve those over the years. It might get to the point where you don't even need my electricity. But whatever it costs, it'll be fine. Don't worry about it."

"That's the best news I've heard in a while." He looked at Vera, who was nodding. "For now, we can run a conduit with an electrical cord in it underneath the ground and sidewalk and have it hook in your garage. It'll be easier to get permission from the township to put that under the sidewalk, I'm sure. And then, if we get a box or something, maybe a separate meter or something, we can pay for all of that, and we can even pay the electric bill, we just...need to put it on your property if that's okay."

"Yes. Absolutely. They can go on my property, and that will be my donation for the healing garden. I'll pay for the electricity. Until I die, and then I'll have to stipulate in my will what's going to happen then, I guess." He gave a rueful smile, which Dominic found himself returning. He really liked Homer. Although he was studious and worked a white-collar job, he found him to be down-to-earth and the kind of man Dominic enjoyed being around.

They chatted a bit more. Homer asked a few questions about what they were doing, and Vera took over the conversation, explaining her designs and what was going to go where.

Homer offered to help, which surprised Dominic, but he said he had just finished a project that day, and his boss had given him the rest of the day off. He worked from home doing computer design for some big, fancy company, from what Dominic understood. Regardless, he appreciated the extra set of hands, and they got a lot more done than what he was expecting.

He and Vera were in the pickup heading home, and he'd just remembered he'd forgotten all about lunch when Homer offered to help, when his phone rang.

He fished it out of his pocket, hoping that the guys that were finishing up the job didn't get hung up on something. He thought they were going to be done by the middle of next week, and he was already lining things up for the next job in northern Michigan.

But when he pulled his phone out, he saw it was Shoshana.

Right then, he probably should have discussed her with his wife, but they'd had such a good day, and he really didn't know what to say, and he was afraid that not only might she be upset that he thought that Shoshana could help her with her career, which he now could see was ridiculous on his part, but he was still trying to figure out how to tell her that he also wished that he wouldn't have worked with Shoshana in the first place. It took him away from his wife's work, from his wife, and perhaps she would have snapped out of her grief better had he been there for her. After all, she was getting better now, as was he, as they spent time together, laughing and healing together.

Because that was what a marriage was supposed to be. Two people relying on each other, not the husband going off keeping himself busy somewhere while leaving the wife to deal with her grief and heartache herself.

Even if she had still wanted to stay home to work through her grief and insisted he work, he should have kept Vera in the loop somehow.

He owed her an apology, but again, they were tired, it had been a long day, a good one, but he thought maybe that conversation would be better had some other time.

He believed in couples communicating, but he also believed in choosing a good time. When they were both tired, and hungry and grumpy, it wasn't a good time for a serious, potentially explosive discussion.

Still, that didn't solve the problem of what to do with Shoshana. For now, he held the phone for just a second and then declined her call.

As he did, he looked across the seat at Vera.

Her head was turning to look out the window, as though she might have been looking at him and was looking away.

He hadn't noticed if she had. Had she seen the name on his phone?

While he didn't think it was a good time for a discussion, if she'd seen the name, he probably ought to say something.

But his brain just wouldn't work. He didn't know what to say, hadn't figured out how he was going to present it to her, and knew it needed to be accompanied by a huge apology.

"We have three more days to work on the garden before we need to leave for Pittsburgh, and if you don't mind, I'm probably going to be there from daylight until dark. I know there's no rush to get it done, but...I'd kind of like to. Now that we have the electricity figured out."

"I understand."

She was upset. He couldn't tell by the tone of her voice, but she started talking while she was still looking out the window. Her head turned to him as he pulled in the drive.

"I'll help you if I can, but I have to finish the design, so probably not tomorrow."

"I have to add that in as I go. I'll probably lay the brickwork first. It'll make it easier to move the wheelbarrow with plants and stuff, and then I'll probably build the fountain."

"That sounds good. You know I'll help with the plants when I get done."

"I knew you would." He grinned at her, and she smiled back, although...was it his imagination, or was her smile not quite reaching her eyes?

Maybe she was as tired as he was. That could be it, too. He was exhausted, she had to be just as tired. They'd pushed themselves hard today. With Homer's help, he didn't want to waste time.

At least she knew now that he wouldn't be meeting her in the morning for their sunrise time, but she would know where he was and not think that he was upset. That was important to him. He wanted to be careful of their relationship. And not take it for granted. It felt like maybe that was the bottom line and what had started everything to begin with.

He had taken for granted that she would be there and that she would be fine, whatever he did, and he hadn't taken her feelings into consideration when he'd made some stupid decisions. Even though he knew better.

And he'd neglected her, off working with another woman when she was struggling.

He would try to keep in mind that he needed to make sure that he spent time with his wife. It shouldn't be hard, there wasn't anyone else in the world he'd rather be with.

Twenty-Five

Vera sat in her chair, her blanket wrapped around her, coffee cup in hand, sunrise brightening the morning sky. The Lord was really putting on a show for her, beautifully so.

Maybe He was trying to talk her out of what she had decided to do.

She was exhausted last night and had barely made a sandwich and grabbed a shower before she collapsed in bed.

She wasn't used to all the work that she had done, and while she enjoyed that kind of work, she kind of liked to ease herself into it a little more.

Her hands had blisters on them, and her knees hurt and creaked when she walked.

But that wasn't what she was thinking about this morning. Although getting out of bed had been painful.

She was old. Just like she had told Dominic.

Last night, Shoshana had called him again. He had told her that he had canceled all of the things that he was doing other than the job in northern Michigan, which she knew Shoshana was not involved in.

So why was she calling her husband?

Vera had dropped in bed last night without checking their scheduling website, to see if he had added her, but she had a premonition. Maybe one that she should just leave well enough alone, but also the feeling that if she checked, she was going to find what she didn't want.

Part of her wanted to know, wanted to get it out in the open, wanted to deal with it, and part of her...wanted to bury her head in the sand and pretend it didn't happen, because after her conversation with Mrs. Calvin, she knew that forgiveness was on the table, even if Dominic cheated, and if he had, he was either doing a really great job of hiding it, or he really wanted her back.

Maybe he wanted both of them.

Was she going to demand that he choose between the two of them?

No, of course not. She wasn't going to do that. That was too much like groveling for her husband.

But Mrs. Calvin had said that her pride shouldn't have anything to do with it.

And she knew that Mrs. Calvin was right. She shouldn't make these decisions based on her pride.

Regardless, as soon as she watched the sunrise, she was going to go into the sunroom, she was going to get the computer up, and she was going to check that out. Premonition or no, it didn't matter. She was going to figure it out once and for all, and then she would figure out what she was going to do. Even if Shoshana wasn't on it, that didn't totally clear her husband, it just meant that he hadn't added her.

The fact that he might have added her was definitely a red flag. She would have to figure out how she was going to confront him and what she was going to say.

But she was getting the cart ahead of the horse.

She sat until every single light of the sunrise faded, and the morning's sun shone yellow in the bright blue sky.

It was time.

Part of her said that she didn't have to do this. She didn't have to confront her husband at all. She could just let it go. Let it be what it was, and let it come out when it did or not at all. But she just wanted to know. She wanted to stop guessing and just know.

So, she walked in, closing the door behind her, folding her blanket up, and putting it in its spot on the living room couch.

Then, she carried a fresh coffee out to the sunroom and flipped open her laptop.

It didn't take long to get to their page, where she could see that all of the jobs that he had had listed before were crossed out. Or had disappeared completely.

The only thing that showed on the schedule was the job that he had told her about in northern Michigan that started the week after next.

And the job that his crew was finishing right now without him.

She went up to the top where it said settings and clicked on the menu. It dropped down, and it took her a minute to figure out which settings she wanted. Permissions.

She clicked on it and held her breath.

There should have been two names. Dominic's and hers.

But there were three.

Shoshana's face, the promotional picture that Vera had seen multiple times before, appeared beside her name.

Vera sat frozen. Unable to think of what she should do. Unable to process, unable to believe what she was seeing.

What was Shoshana doing on Dominic's calendar? The one he shared with her, and her alone?

And how could her husband add someone to the calendar and think she wouldn't notice?

Except she hadn't. Obviously. She hadn't thought to check, maybe that's what he was counting on, that she considered him an honest to a fault, upright to the point where he couldn't lie kind of person, and wouldn't. Maybe he was so confident in his reputation, prideful perhaps. The kind of pride that went before a fall.

Although, as soon as she thought that, she thought immediately that she was dealing with pride as well. She was the one who was too proud to grovel for her husband. She was the one who was going to allow her pride to make the decision. She was too proud to be married to a man who would cheat. Was that it?

Maybe she was too proud to continue to stay married to a cheater.

Although, there was nothing in the Bible that required that. But forgiveness *was* required, and forgiveness meant humbling herself, to the point where she looked to God to deal with her husband, not herself.

It all seemed kind of convoluted in her head, but she knew that pride was bad, even though the world said she needed to hold her head up and make herself proud, or whatever it was that the world would tell her to do. Definitely not accept treatment like this, to have more self-respect, yeah. The world prized self-respect and self-esteem. She needed to have enough self-esteem to not allow people to treat her like that, but that wasn't what the Bible said. The Bible talked about pride being wrong and how the humble person was lifted up by God. God would take care of her, if she were humble.

But she was borrowing trouble. She had no idea why Shoshana's name was on there, and speculating about it was doing no good.

She swallowed, clicked off on the calendar, and took a deep breath.

She needed to sit down at her desk and make the designs that had been in her head all day yesterday. Yesterday when she was innocent and didn't know what her husband was doing. Yesterday, when they were laughing at Trent's grave and holding hands. Yesterday, when they were working together the way they had for years, him reading her mind and her doing everything she could to lighten his load, anticipate his needs, and be a blessing.

That was yesterday.

Today, today was much different.

Lord, please help me keep my mouth shut until I can say things kindly and with grace. Please help me not to judge my husband more harshly than I judge myself. Please help me to submit to Your authority and Your will in this. I... I want to throttle someone right now, although I'm not sure whether it's Shoshana or Dominic. Maybe both. But I know that's not what You want for me. You want kindness. You want grace, You want compassion, You want...love.

She thought about that last word. What that entailed, how big the scope of that last word was. She had pledged to *love* her husband.

Love meant seeing no wrong, love meant believing the best. Love meant serving without expecting anything in return. Love believed the best, hoped for it, worked for it. *That* was love.

Twenty-Six

The days before the tenth anniversary celebration in Pittsburgh went by quickly, much to Dominic's surprise. He was back working, doing what he loved, and doing it with the one he loved.

Working on Vera's design was a no-brainer. It was familiar and beloved, and maybe it was because it was his wife, but he took extra care with the design. He wanted to show her off in the very best way that he could. And he loved that they were able to collaborate like they were and could work together. It wasn't something that he should take for granted, and he wouldn't, not ever again.

Each day, he was out working first. She came a little later, although the first day, she didn't come until midafternoon. She showed him the designs, and he had to admit they were brilliant. He immediately ordered the supplies that he needed, after he configured it, and they were delivered the second morning.

They weren't going to get the whole thing done, but it was going to come together very nicely before they left.

Vera seemed to understand his need to throw himself into the work and get it finished.

Neither one of them considered pacing themselves. For some reason, there was an urgency between them, maybe because of finally going to visit Trent's grave and now wanting to do something to honor him, or maybe it was just for themselves and their relationship.

Dominic knew better than to try to question it. He wasn't very good in that area, but he did know that there was a need to get it done.

By the day before their flight was booked, almost everything was finished, and he had just completed everything he needed to in order to start the water fountain.

It was actually a waterfall, which split off, with one side curving around the crosses, where they were displayed, thirteen of them in an asymmetrical pattern, with thirteen plants each of four different species of flowers planted around them, two that would bloom in spring, one for summer, and one for fall.

Thirteen of each plant. In the same asymmetrical pattern as the crosses.

The second stream went down a waterfall and fell into a pool that was shallow and still. Like a reflecting pool.

It was a brilliant design, and he couldn't be more proud of his wife for coming up with it.

"I think that's it. If it doesn't work, I'm going to be disappointed, but I'll probably have to operate, and we're not going to have time."

"We probably should have quit a while ago. We need to leave here at three o'clock tomorrow morning if we're going to make our flight at seven in Ann Arbor."

"Yeah. You're right. But it's going to bug me the whole time we're gone if this doesn't work."

He didn't know why he thought it might not work. Maybe because they put it together so quickly, or maybe because he hadn't put a whole lot of fountains in.

He really wanted to see if it all worked. They hadn't gotten permission from the township, since the meeting wasn't until the next week, but they had an extension cord they could run across the sidewalk and plug into Homer's garage. He half expected Homer to come out and take a look, but he imagined that his boss had probably assigned him a new project, and Homer was knee-deep in it the way Dominic would have been.

"How about I plug it in, and you stand there and watch?" Vera said, and he knew she said it to try to spare him or to allow him to be the one to see whether it worked first.

"Actually, if you don't mind standing there and seeing if it works, I'll plug it in. Just... If it doesn't, break it to me gently, please."

"Of course. I'll do that," she said with an easy smile.

She had been sweet and friendly the entire time, the Vera that he'd always loved working with, only...just a little different.

He kinda thought maybe their camaraderie during the day would translate to her no longer curling up in a ball and sleeping on her side of the bed at night, but it hadn't.

He supposed there were a lot of things they still needed to talk about, but baby steps. At least they were talking. There was that.

Maybe, on the trip they would find some time. Not in the airplane—too many people around—and not at the anniversary celebration, but they were supposed to have a really nice Airbnb. Maybe there. Maybe they could talk... He should have planned something romantic. Made reservations at a nice restaurant or something. He was an idiot. Instead of romancing his wife, what was he doing? Working her to the bone, from daylight to dusk, on a landscaping project.

Except, he was pretty sure she was into it too.

He walked across the sidewalk and grabbed the end of the extension cord which was lying down beside the plug just inside the garage.

"Are you ready?" he called across the sidewalk.

"Whenever you are."

Once upon a time, back in their younger days, she might have teased him about hiding behind a rock so that he wouldn't be hurt in the explosion, just in case.

But there was no such teasing today. He wasn't sure if it was because she was tired, or because she had matured, or maybe...there was something else. He couldn't deny that he felt like something was a little bit off, but considering all the things that were between them, he supposed it was normal. Hopefully they could talk it out and figure it out.

Taking a deep breath, he took the orange extension cord and shoved it into the socket.

At first, he didn't hear the pump, and then he could just hear the low hum, and then...he could hear the water.

"It works!" Vera called, and a couple seconds later, she came running out from behind a tall grass plant. "Come see it! It's awesome!"

And that was the old Vera, her face shining with excitement and happiness and pride in him. It was obvious that she gave him all the credit for it, even though the design had been hers.

"I can hear the water," he said as he crossed the sidewalk and took the path into the garden. Eventually they wanted to put a wrought iron fence around the entire thing, but...details they would add later.

They had the bones done now, Vera might even add a few more plants here and there, depending on how things looked, or she might design a little bit more for the back end. She told him that she had left the back a little lower than what she might have normally, because she thought they would have room, and maybe there would be some benches a person could sit in and look out across the lake. It would require a little bit more excavation work, and they were both just happy to get what they had finished done.

He came around the grass and walked the path toward the waterfall and the special memorial with the crosses.

"I don't know what it is, but the sound of water is always soothing. Waves, a creek, a river, whatever. It's just..."

"Even looking at a pond, a small lake, one that doesn't have waves, just seeing the reflections on the water, feeling that peace, it just...there's always something about it."

"I agree. Water doesn't have to be moving to be inspiring."

"Exactly," she said, glancing at him with a smile like he had given her the words that she was looking for.

He loved it when they could read each other's minds like that.

They stood watching it for a little bit.

"Are we going to leave it plugged in?"

"We have to talk to Homer about that, I think. If the extension cord was under the sidewalk, I would feel like we're good, but since it's not..."

"Hey! Did you guys finish?" Homer's voice reached them over the murmur of the water.

They both turned, with Dominic putting his arm around his wife.

Maybe it was his imagination that she might have stiffened just a bit, but then she relaxed into him. He wondered about that.

But he didn't have time to think about it because she said, "We did. You have good eyes."

"My office is right above the garden, and I can look out and see the garage and your healing garden. Which, I have to say, is a nice benefit."

"I hope so. It's going to take a little bit of care at first, some watering and that type of thing," Vera said.

"We're going to be going away tomorrow, and we're not coming back for a couple of days, would you be okay if we left the fountain plugged in?"

"Sure. That's not a problem. It's going to stay plugged in normally, right?"

"Yeah. I guess I was thinking because the extension cord is going above the sidewalk, it'll just take someone keeping an eye on it and making sure that no one comes around and unplugs it, walks away with the cord."

"Sure, I can do that," Homer said easily.

"I don't think anyone will probably bother it, but you never know. People come here from all over, parking at the end of the street and walking the path to the bluffs. Most of the time, they're just folks who want to enjoy the beauty of nature, but every once in a while, you have a couple of bad actors."

"Yeah. They're the ones who ruin it for everyone, but I'll keep an eye on things. Like I said, I can see it easily from my office window, and it won't be a problem to keep an eye on it all day long, although if there's going to be any mischief, it'll probably be at night."

"Eventually we want to put a wrought iron fence around it, but not that that would keep anyone out. It'll just make it a little bit harder for them to get in."

"That would be a nice touch too," Homer said.

Dominic wouldn't have minded standing there and talking, but he said, "I know I'm tired, and my wife has to be exhausted as well."

"Every day, you guys were up working before I got out of bed, and you worked until dark as far as I could tell. Not that I was spying on you. That's the way my window faces."

"You're right. You got us figured out. We're guilty."

"I'm sure you're both tired. I'll head back over to the house, but I might bring my mom over later and show it to her. She's going to love it."

"Please tell Gertie I said hi. And maybe once I get back, we can figure out a time to have tea."

"I'll pick a time when she knows who I'm talking about and let her know." There was a little bit of a shadow in Homer's face as he said that, and again, Dominic wondered about a man who would sacrifice so much to care for his mom as Homer walked away.

It would be easier for Homer if he had a woman beside him. A wife, like Vera. Although, there weren't a whole lot of wives like Vera around. Someone who was more interested in others than in herself. Someone who loved unselfishly, who saw his dream, and who helped him achieve it.

He'd been blessed, over and over, and he hoped he appreciated that.

He tugged on her hand a little, and they turned, facing the waterfall again.

"What you did with those crosses is amazing," he said.

"You're the one who came up with the idea for them."

"I was just making the crosses, just something to do with my hands while I processed everything that we had talked about at the graveside. It's sad to think of so many children dying. I know some of them are more than one hundred years old, but it's still sad."

"That's just a small, small drop in the bucket. So much suffering in the world."

"When I get to heaven, I'm going to have a few words to say to Eve," he said, squeezing her shoulder.

"Really? You think it's Eve's fault?"

"She was the one who was deceived by the serpent," he said.

"But Adam wasn't deceived. Adam deliberately took the fruit." She snorted. "That means that Eve was an accident, but Adam sinned deliberately. That's what caused the fall."

"Don't you understand? Adam took the fruit because he couldn't stand to be separated from Eve."

Yeah, his wife had never thought about that before, he was sure as she searched his eyes, trying to come up with an argument for that, but he knew she couldn't. Neither one of them could prove what they were saying, because the Bible just didn't say, other than that Eve was deceived, that was a fact. Whether Adam was deceived, or whether he deliberately took it because he loved Eve, and whatever punishment was going to happen, he didn't want to happen to her alone. Or whether he took it with visions of glory, Dominic couldn't say.

But he wanted to believe that Adam loved his wife the same way that Dominic loved Vera. Like she was half of his whole, the half that he needed in order to be complete. The one he wanted beside him, no matter what he was doing. The one he turned to when things didn't go right. And the one he turned to when things did go right.

She was the one. And if it meant that he had to take the apple and instigate the fall of man, in order to continue to be with her, he supposed he would choose to do that.

Twenty-Seven

Vera did not think three AM was a good time for anyone.

When a person traveled as much as she and Dominic did, getting up at three AM was not atypical. It wasn't natural, either.

As they came down into Raspberry Ridge, to turn right to go out the road starting on their way toward Ann Arbor, Vera looked up and could just see the glow of the fountain.

Once the plants had grown some, a person wouldn't be able to see it at all.

"I'm glad you suggested putting lights in the fountain. I especially like the backlit waterfall."

"I know it was a little bit more time and effort, but I really thought it would be pretty. And I like that we can turn them off if we want to. Maybe we'll end up not using them much at all, but they're there if we want them."

"I suppose we could put a fancier system in."

"It would cost more. But yeah, something that could be computer-controlled, particularly with the fountain."

Vera didn't say much more. Her sluggish brain was slowly reminding her of the fact that she had seen the evidence that she had been afraid she was going to see a few days ago.

But she wasn't going to jump to conclusions about what exactly was going on.

But she just couldn't seem to find a good time to talk about it. They'd been in such a rush to get the garden in, and now, she didn't think she wanted to talk about it on the way to the celebration. Just in case what he said wasn't what she wanted to hear, she didn't want that to dampen things for her in Pittsburgh, and she also didn't want to have to try to struggle to get through it, when she wanted to grab a plastic knife and stab her husband with it.

Hopefully things wouldn't go to that extreme, but there was the potential for her to find out some really big information, information that could change her entire life, and it probably wasn't a good idea to do it before she was going to be in front of cameras and interviewers, especially if she hoped to increase her visibility and possibly gain some new clients.

With that thought in her head, she sipped at her coffee and watched as the eastern sky slowly lightened.

They would be at the airport before sunrise, but once they got through TSA, Ann Arbor had a beautiful place where she could watch the sunrise and wait for their plane.

"You've been really quiet," Dominic said, after they'd been on the road for an hour and a half and were just about to hit the traffic of Ann Arbor. Not that there would be that much at this time of morning.

"I know you don't enjoy talking in the morning," she said, which wasn't exactly the reason that she'd been quiet, but it was probably another good one. Dominic didn't exactly enjoy early-morning chitchat, and confronting him about something that was potentially explosive in their relationship was probably not a good idea at three AM.

"Thank you for being considerate. I'm feeling like I've finally woken up," he said, looking over at her and grinning a bit.

The dash lights glowed on the strong lines of his face, emphasizing his clean-shaven cheeks and his jaw that could smile easily or be set in a hard line of determination.

But not unkindness. That was not something that she ever saw in her husband.

Or dishonesty. That was something else she'd never seen.

Both of them had brought a carry-on bag, since they were only staying in Pittsburgh for one night. The celebration was at 2 PM today. Then they'd eat and go to their Airbnb, which, from the pictures, looked like it was going to be really nice. The organizers of the event had put them up and paid for their stay, in return for them coming to the celebration and agreeing to say a few words.

"Have you thought about what you're going to say?" Dominic asked as he made the familiar turns into the Ann Arbor airport.

It wasn't a huge one, and they probably hadn't needed to arrive two hours early, but neither one of them wanted to be late, and neither of them wanted to miss their plane, of course.

"No. I really haven't. Typically I don't. I just go up to the microphone and kind of speak from my heart. I know that sounds cheesy, but it's true."

"I usually have a few little things written down on a piece of paper, and I say the same thing almost every time."

"This is our first grand anniversary. Are you going to change it up a little?" She tried to smile and be friendly. She could be wrong, and she didn't want to waste any of her life being unkind, especially if it was for no reason. Even if he had done something wrong, that did not give her license to not treat him with kindness and respect.

"I probably will. Maybe I'll work on it on the airplane." He put his turn signal on and followed the signs for long-term parking. Sometimes in the winter, they parked a little closer, but she didn't mind walking, in fact, she appreciated the fact that she got to stretch her legs and exercise a bit before they were cramped on an airplane. Their flight would go to Chicago, and from there, they'd fly to Pittsburgh.

"You're the one who's so good at knowing what to say. Maybe you'll give me a hand."

"I suppose I could." If she were being catty, there was a part of her that wanted to say, *maybe you should ask Shoshana about it*. But...that was ridiculous. She wasn't in junior high anymore. If she wanted to talk about Shoshana, she would bring it up like a mature adult and discuss the issue at hand.

Since she had already predetermined that this was not a good time, she was not going to think of snide remarks to say, nor was she going to allow such a thing to escape her lips.

"You don't sound too thrilled about it."

"I don't mind. And I will happily help you, but you do want your thoughts to be your thoughts and not mine. I suppose I can ask you a few questions to prompt you a little, if that works."

"Yeah. You're right. My speech should be my thoughts, and I do have a few thoughts about it." He grinned. "I'll talk to you if I get stuck."

"All right."

She didn't know what she was going to say. Normally she would say something about how amazing her husband was, and how much she loved working with him, and how much she hoped this garden would continue to soothe and help people.

But today, she didn't feel like saying a whole lot of nice things about her husband, and maybe she would focus more on the soothing and helping aspect of the garden. Perhaps she would even mention Trent.

She felt a little less sensitive about even thinking his name. Definitely the last couple of weeks had been healing in that regard. Her marriage had started to come around, and she as a person had started to come around. She felt like she was emerging from a fog.

She didn't want to be set back. Maybe she would never say anything about Shoshana.

They parked, and both of them got their carry-on roller bags out of the back, closed the trunk, locked the car, and started to walk.

Dominic reached down and slid his fingers through hers, linking them together.

Part of her wished she would have thought to put her suitcase in her left hand, but she hadn't. And now she was walking hand in hand with her husband, like they had done so many times before.

They hadn't flown thousands of times, or even hundreds, but they'd definitely flown a dozen times out of this airport if not two or three.

It seemed like a lot over the years.

She'd slowed down after their son was born, and he'd been through this airport multiple times without her.

In the last year and a half, she'd flown some without him, but not much. Just to places like the garden that had just opened in Cleveland, since he was already on another job.

But this was her normal, her husband beside her, holding her hand.

And if she'd let it, it would feel good, and bright, and perfect. The way it always had, and she just hadn't taken the time to examine her feelings and appreciate how perfect it was.

Now that she knew, knew what a wonderful man her husband was, but how slippery and frail and delicate a relationship could be, especially one that wasn't getting regular care, she understood that walking into the airport while holding hands with her husband of more than a decade wasn't something to be taken for granted.

They'd go in, and he would manage her luggage and his as they went through TSA, giving her freedom to deal with her purse and her shoes, and then when they were loading, he would take his bag and her bag, putting them both in the overhead bins. While all she had to do was get into her seat and put her seat belt on, stowing her purse.

He would ask her if she was thirsty and get her a drink while they were waiting, or something to eat if it was mealtime and they were hungry. He would wait at the restroom while she went. Or sit with her bags or find a place where there was a restroom nearby if he thought she was going to have to go.

The entire time she was pregnant, he never complained about the number of times he had to stop and wait for her to pee.

If she had to use the restroom on the plane, he'd ask if she was comfortable walking back, and if she wasn't, he'd go with her.

"Have I ever told you how much I like to travel with you?" Vera asked, looking over at Dominic as they walked toward the TSA line, a little smile on her face. It didn't matter whether he made mistakes or not, she still loved him. And she hadn't appreciated him like he deserved.

"I don't think so. Why? Did you take a few flights by yourself and realize that it was nicer to have me along?"

"Yeah. Something like that. You always get me a drink if I need it, make sure to watch my bag so I can use the restroom, it's...nice to have a partner."

"That's kind of why we got married, isn't it? To have a life partner?"

She nodded.

Maybe there was a shadow that passed over his eyes, but they were in the airport now and heading to TSA, which was not busy at all.

She read somewhere that four AM was the busiest time of day for an airport, but Ann Arbor was just a regional airport, and if it had a busy time, the crowd had dispersed.

"This is much nicer than trying to go through TSA at Chicago, that's for sure," Dominic said.

"Or Pittsburgh. It won't be nearly so nice coming back."

"You're right about that. Although...there's something about Pittsburgh that I really like. I guess I don't think of the inconvenience as much when I'm enjoying it and liking it."

"They do have nice shops."

"I've never noticed," he said, and they grinned together, standing in line and pulling their ID and phones out so they could scan their boarding passes.

"You two are so adorable," an older lady said as her head popped up to the side of the line, her blue eyes twinkling and her gnarled hand sitting on one of the stands that held the tape to keep the lines in order.

"Um, thank you?" Vera said, unsure where that came from.

"I walked in behind you the last few hundred yards or so. You guys were holding hands and talking and laughing, and I see your rings, so you're obviously married. It's unusual to find a married couple who actually seems to enjoy being with each other." She paused for a minute, and a sly grin came over her face. "Especially this time of morning," she said, then she just smiled and said, "Have a great day," and rolled her luggage toward the baggage check area.

"That was unusual," Dominic said as she left, silence falling between them.

"Yeah. I wasn't quite sure what in the world she was saying at first."

"We've never had anyone do that to us before."

"We look a little older now," she said.

"Battle scarred. Maybe it's unbelievable that two people who have been married for a decade still hold hands."

"She mentioned it. I suppose..." She almost didn't say what she was going to say, then she realized that she had encouraged other people to talk about him, but she hadn't. "If Trent were here, he'd be between us, and we didn't always walk around holding hands whenever he was around. He seemed to steal both of our attention."

"He did. Maybe that isn't necessarily a good thing, since children come and they go, although usually they graduate from high school and college and eventually move out of the house."

"Eventually." She nodded, even though it had been a little bit sad because what he hadn't said was that Trent had been taken from them a little early.

"I don't regret the attention we paid to him, but it is important to, like you said, pay attention to your marriage because hopefully that will be something that you still have after the kids are grown and gone." He did not say dead and gone.

That wasn't the way it was supposed to be.

They made it through TSA and found their gate, and Vera used the restroom while Dominic sat with their bags. She came back, but he shook his head when she asked if he needed to go.

They sat there together side by side, their bags in front of them, their joined hands between them.

She loved this man. She loved him. Love covered a multitude of sins. That's what the Bible said. Which meant, when you love someone, you shouldn't notice their faults, their flaws, their mistakes, you should just see their good and focus on that. And you weren't prideful, it said in Corinthians 13, which is what she struggled with. She wanted to demand his punishment, demand what he owed her, but that wasn't right. To demand something from someone else. The Bible said they were supposed to be servants, givers, not demanding people who insisted on their own way.

She was mulling that over as the countdown on the screen got lower and lower until the airport employees finally came to the speaker and announced boarding would begin.

"You know what group we are?" Dominic asked, and she smiled. He never thought about things until they were right on him, and he needed it now.

"Group five. We're after all the important people go."

He grinned. "They just don't know who you are," he said, giving her that lopsided, roguish grin that always made her heart twirl.

Like it was doing now.

"I'm going to the restroom. Do you need to go?"

He would let her go first, or if she wanted to go second, he would let her do whatever she wanted. He was...a good man, he wasn't bossy or controlling, he didn't insist that she had to do what he wanted, and he didn't complain when what she needed or wanted wasn't convenient for him.

She'd married a good man.

"No thank you. You go ahead."

Tomorrow, their plane didn't leave until one in the afternoon. They could have a leisurely morning.

Or a late night. Whichever.

Tonight would be a good time to talk. She would get it all off her chest, and she would do it with the spirit of forgiveness. And love.

Whatever he had done, she wasn't perfect either. And she would try to be kind and reasonable. But she wasn't the kind of person who could just not know. As much as she didn't really want to know, she needed to.

But tonight would be soon enough. And in the meantime, she would enjoy traveling with the best man in the world. He made things fun, easy for her, and he made her feel like she was important to him by always giving her deference.

As the line moved slowly forward, her phone rang.

She glanced at it. "It's Peggy. Let me grab it, okay?"

"Sure. We can step out of line. It's not like somebody's going to take our seats," he said, moving their baggage aside, as she gave him another apologetic look, which he shrugged off with a grin, and swiped at her phone.

She loved that he didn't care, encouraged her to do what she wanted, which was answer the call of her friend, just in case it was something important.

"Hello," she said, walking a little distance away from the line so her conversation wouldn't bother anyone.

"Vera, I thought I might have missed you. I know your flight leaves early."

"We're in line to board right now."

"Oh. I'm sorry to bother you, but I really wanted you to know this. I just found out, late last night, and I knew you'd already be in bed, because of time differences and everything."

"You know it's okay for you to call me anytime."

"I wanted to talk to you before you took off too."

"It must be the middle of the night for you," Vera said, looking at her watch and trying to do the math in her head. "Or at least 4:30."

"Every once in a while, the spoiled girl who does nothing but lie around and get pampered has to get up for a few minutes."

It was funny that Vera couldn't tell the difference between Peggy at 4:30 in the morning and Peggy at 4:30 in the afternoon. Peggy was Peggy.

"Anyway, Shoshana is going to be there today. I saw that on the news last night. I was flipping through the Internet, looking at Pittsburgh news, just looking to see if they were going to say your name or say anything about you, and all the news was about her. I think that was her intent. I actually heard someone saying that she and Dominic have another project in the works. It was heavily hinted that it was going to be announced tomorrow."

"Are you serious?" Vera said, a little shocked that Shoshana would do that. Shocked that Dominic would hide it from her. But she had been deliberately not asking, so she kind of deserved it if he was, but after thinking about how kind he had been, would he really be planning on not saying anything?

"Thank you so much for telling me. It would have been worse to get caught flat-footed, although I don't know what I'm going to do about it."

"I don't either. Other than, I know you're giving a few remarks, so... you might want to get together with Dominic and make sure that the two of you are a rock-solid team so she can't split you guys up. It looks to me like that's what she's trying to do."

That could be. Dominic might be too nice to have told her to back off, but she couldn't really respect a man who was too nice to defend his wife and left her vulnerable.

That really wasn't Dominic, although she knew that Dominic didn't have a mean bone in his body and wouldn't be unkind unless the situation absolutely demanded it, in which case, he would handle it the way it needed to be handled. But he probably would be especially reluctant to be unkind to a woman.

Vera had to tamp down the anger that rose in her chest. After all, she was his wife. He shouldn't be reluctant to tell Shoshana to go bug off. That she was overstepping her bounds in a big and irritating way.

Of course, Dominic might not want to ruin his relationship with

Shoshana, just in case he was planning on working with her in the future, although if Shoshana was announcing a job, Dominic had told her he had canceled everything except for the job in northern Michigan.

"Thanks again. I appreciate you getting up at this crazy hour in the morning, just to give me a phone call and let me know."

"That's what friends are for, kiddo. You be careful. I love you."

"Love you too, Peggy. Go back to bed and get some more rest."

They laughed and hung up.

Vera wished that she would have made time at some point to talk to Dominic about Shoshana, so it wasn't so upsetting to her now, but again, she thought of the words to that old hymn, *Turn your eyes upon Jesus, look full in His wonderful face, and the things of earth will grow strangely dim, in the light of His glory and grace.*

She pondered that last line. *The things of earth will grow strangely dim, in the light of His glory and grace.*

This life wasn't about her, it was about Jesus. It wasn't about Shoshana, and it wasn't about Vera, and it wasn't about the competition between them and Shoshana taking Vera's attention today at the celebration and trying to catch the eye of her husband.

It was about Jesus. It was about Vera acting in such a way that she looked different from the rest of the world. Could she do it?

She honestly wasn't sure.

Twenty-Nine

Dominic sat on the plane after it had taken off from Chicago, his head leaning back on the headrest, thinking.

He had jotted down a few things that he wanted to say on his phone app, but most of what he wanted to say involved Vera.

And then he had started thinking about doing kind things for her and was annoyed with himself for not making reservations somewhere nice for this evening.

He probably wouldn't get anything nice at this point, and he couldn't do it in front of her anyway, and he definitely couldn't do it on the plane.

But he was thinking about doing kind things for his wife, and how... he had been thinking about doing kind things to help repair the relationship, but that wasn't really the right reason to do kind things for his wife.

He should do them because she was his wife. Because he was a Christian. Because doing kind things for others should be second nature to Christians. Thinking about them, considering them, making sure that he put them first, and his wife first of all.

He had been tempted to bring up Shoshana on the way in to the airport, but he hadn't wanted to ruin the day. If it had hurt her feelings that he had worked with her, and she didn't see anything good that would come out of it, or that good didn't outweigh the bad in her opinion, it wasn't going to be a good conversation for her, and he wanted them both to have a good trip in, since they would barely land in Pittsburgh before they needed to drive straight to the celebration. They would probably get there half an hour early, so they would have time to grab a bite to eat if they wanted to.

They should be able to go straight from the celebration and check in if they wanted to, although she might be hungry.

But this elusive thought, the one he couldn't quite grab a hold of, about doing kind things, particularly for his wife. She had mentioned how nice it was to fly with him, and it wasn't because he was doing anything unusual. He was just doing what he always did. Except, he hadn't been doing that for the last eighteen months, since they hadn't been spending time together.

In order to do kind things for someone, he almost had to be with her, although he supposed he could send her gifts from afar. But long-distance relationships were notoriously difficult for a reason. And he had deliberately been away.

Well, this is what he came home to when he went off, nursing his wounds, keeping himself busy, working with his wife's competitor and lifting that woman up, helping her, instead of his wife. He leaned his head back against his headrest and closed his eyes. He'd made a mess of things.

"How long have you been married?"

Dominic lifted his head and opened his eyes to see a lady from across the aisle looking directly at him.

"Me?" he said, having been lost in thought.

"Yeah. You and your wife are so cute together."

This was the second person who told him that today. That was so weird. After having never heard that before in his life, to hear it twice, and in one morning. Before lunchtime no less. Before breakfast.

"I saw how you put her carry-on bag up for her. And then you put up your own. You carried them both on the plane too. That was really sweet of you. My husband, rest his soul, used to do the same for me. But I hardly ever see that anymore."

"Maybe that's partly Vera," he said, thinking that actually it probably was. "Some women wouldn't want to have a man carrying their bags. They would insist they could do it themselves."

"That's a good point, but it makes me think that your relationship is just as much you as her, since you're deferring to her, and obviously, that's part of what it takes to have a good marriage. To lift the other one up."

"That's right. It is."

"Where're you headed?" the woman said, and while he didn't typically mind talking to people, talking across the aisle was a little awkward.

Beside him, Vera sat looking out the window from the middle seat. It was funny, he liked the aisle seat, and she liked the window seat, so when she booked the tickets, she booked an aisle seat for him and she took the middle. When he booked the tickets, he booked a window seat for her and he took the middle.

A person could tell by looking where they were sitting as to who booked the tickets.

"We're going to Pittsburgh to go to the ten-year celebration of a garden that my wife and I designed and built together."

"My goodness, that's where I'm going too. The Pittsburgh Memorial Garden?" the woman asked, as though to confirm that there weren't two memorial garden celebrations happening later that day in Pittsburgh.

"That's the one. We'll see you there."

"You guys are the ones who designed and built that?"

"We are."

"So you're Vera and Dominic Miller! I've... I've heard of you. I've gotten so much pleasure out of your garden. When my husband, Randel Bomar, died, I spent hours sitting in the garden, watching the reflections of the water, how the grasses waved, how it reflected the landscape of Pittsburgh and allowed a person to enjoy all of the various things, the hills, the skyline, and especially the river." The woman's hands fiddled with the purse on her lap. "We have beautiful gardens at our private residence, but they just don't soothe my soul like yours do."

Dominic tried to contain his surprise. Randel Bomar was a

billionaire, who was known as one of the richest men on earth. He had started in oil and switched to computer chips and had invested in several start-ups that had solidified his immense wealth.

He couldn't believe that his widow was flying coach with him, on her way to Pittsburgh. But she did seem like an unassuming woman.

Unless she didn't inherit his billions, and he gave them to someone else. Billionaires could be weird like that, in Dominic's experience anyway.

"I'm sorry for your loss. My wife and I actually lost our son. It's been almost a year and a half, and the loss is still difficult. We just built a garden near our home, in our hometown of Raspberry Ridge. We...are glad that our designs brought you comfort, and hopefully they will bring others comfort as well."

The lady nodded. "Raspberry Ridge. I'm from Chicago, but I think that's up near Blueberry Beach, isn't it?"

"Yeah. Just a little north of that, up the lakeshore some."

"Interesting. I'll have to go see it. I've become quite a fan of your work. You and your wife."

"Thank you. I....wasn't expecting to find a fan on the airplane," Dominic said.

Technically, he wasn't expecting to find a fan anywhere, but details.

"Well, I won't make you talk to me the whole trip, but it was really nice to find that out about you and to see you guys have such a great relationship off-camera. It's not just for show, it's the real deal. That's what Randel and I had. The real deal." The lady let out a breath. "He had a couple of affairs. You might have heard about that."

"I guess I did."

"People wondered how I could forgive him, and they assumed it was because of the money."

Her eyes turned to his, and they turned sharp and shrewd. "It wasn't about the money."

She gave a sly smile. "I would have gotten half of everything we had, had I divorced him, and it was quite a substantial amount, far more than I would ever need." She rolled her eyes. "It was because I loved him. He wasn't perfect, in fact, far from it, but I loved him. And I'm not sure why he made the mistakes he made. Maybe he allowed himself to do things that he shouldn't have or to be places with people who were too tempting, I don't know. I was devastated, don't get me wrong, but I just couldn't imagine my life without him. And he wanted me. I guess that was all I needed to know."

Dominic nodded his head, unsure what to say. What did a man say to that? He didn't have any answers, didn't have any advice, didn't have any comments. Although he understood what she was saying about allowing himself into situations where he shouldn't.

When Dominic was away from Vera, even for the last eighteen months, when their relationship wasn't the greatest, he didn't go out somewhere alone where he might encounter a single woman who would be tempting. Shoshana had invited him for dinner, but he wouldn't have accepted. He had never gone out to eat with someone of the opposite sex who was not his wife.

He couldn't do that to his wife.

The food cart came through at that time, and when he looked over again, Mrs. Bomar had her head back and was snoring slightly.

"Is that *the* Mrs. Bomar? The billionaire's wife?" Vera said softly from his side.

"The very one, or so she claims. We're going to be seeing her later today, at the anniversary celebration. She's a fan of ours."

"You're kidding," Vera said. "I mean, I heard her say that, but I thought that was nuts."

"I know. I wasn't expecting to meet a fan, not on the airplane, not anywhere. It's not like we have mobs of people bombarding us everywhere we go."

"And we don't have to run from the paparazzi," she said with a twinkle in her eye.

No. There was no one for him but his Vera.

He leaned over, placed a kiss on her forehead, and he knew he surprised her, but he didn't care. He loved her, and he wanted her to know.

Thirty

Vera took a deep breath, trying to tell herself to relax.

Normally these things did not bother her at all, and most of the time, she enjoyed them. It was an opportunity to meet and greet local officials and ordinary citizens and make new friends.

The extrovert part of her enjoyed chatting with people, laughing, and talking about her design. A lot of times, people asked interesting questions and were deeply interested in her methods and how she worked. It was fun and flattering to mingle with people who thought so much of her.

But today was different. Today...not only marked the first time in years that she and Dominic were together at one of these, but it was the first time they were together since Dominic had worked with someone else, and that "someone else" was going to be there.

Yeah. It was Shoshana that was making Vera nervous.

Lord, You know what's going to happen, when I have no clue. Help me to keep my eyes on You.

Remembering the song that had been going through her head helped her think about keeping her eyes on Jesus: *and the things of earth will grow strangely dim.*

That was what she was going to cling to to get through it. This didn't matter, not in the long run, not making her look good anyway. What mattered was that Jesus would be glorified.

And if that meant Vera needed to stand back and allow Shoshana and Dominic to have the spotlight, even when it was "her" day, and she was supposed to be sharing it with her husband... Jesus knew, and Jesus wouldn't be glorified by her grabbing what was hers and demanding it. He would be glorified by her stepping back and allowing him to work in the situation.

There was a verse that went through her mind as well. Stand still, and see the salvation of the Lord, which he will shew to you today.

Stand still. She didn't have to do anything, she didn't have to fight, she didn't have to scrap, she didn't have to fuss or be jealous or demand her way. She could just rest in God, stand still, and see the salvation of the Lord.

Lord, I can't wait to see what You're going to do, she thought, feeling immediately better.

"You're smiling. You've been so quiet and withdrawn on this trip. I wouldn't think getting up an hour earlier in the morning would make that big of a difference, but I've been a little worried about you. Are you sick?" Dominic looked across the console of the rental car, a little bit of concern in his eyes, but relief there as well, to see her smile.

What did it say that she had smiled so little that he was worried about her?

"I've had a lot of things on my mind. And I think you and I have a long talk overdue, but I'm hoping things will soon be back to normal." She nodded her head as she spoke and watched his eyes as hope entered them, and it made her feel guilty. Like that was what he wanted all along, and he was just waiting for her.

"I didn't make reservations for dinner, but I can."

"We can just grab something quick and go straight to the Airbnb. It looks like it has a beautiful view, and I bet we'll enjoy it."

"I bet we'll enjoy it too, beautiful view or not. As long as I'm with you, I know I'm going to be having a good time."

"Same." So much the same.

They pulled into the parking area. Pittsburgh was hilly, with crazily arranged streets that didn't always make a whole lot of sense. She'd worked in the city long enough that she was familiar with some of the odd ways streets turned and twisted, up hills and down, with bridges everywhere.

It was a beautiful city though, set on the banks of the Allegheny and Monongahela rivers, which converged to form the Ohio.

The three rivers, which were all beautiful in their own right, helped to make Pittsburgh unique.

"I'm kind of glad we found this spot. Sometimes parking is a little challenging in this city."

"It's not flat like so many of the Western towns. But that gives it character."

"Yeah. Unless you're driving, and then it gives headaches."

She laughed. "Duly noted. My husband wants me to drive on the way home."

"He wants no such thing. He was just making a joke. Driving you around is an honor," he said, winking.

"Like you're not going to," she said, laughing.

It was the kind of thing that they used to tease each other about a good bit, always finding something to laugh about and always making sure that their complaints were not excessive and onerous.

"All right, here's to the first of many ten-year anniversary celebrations of the gardens we designed. Let's go," he said as they met around the front of the car, him holding his hand out, offering it to her.

She slipped her fingers into his, the familiar feeling wrapping around her heart just as much, making her feel connected to her husband, in a way she hadn't for a long time. She would have thought, and actually told Peggy, that she didn't know whether their relationship was repairable, and now, she felt like the only way the relationship wouldn't be back to thriving, stronger than ever, would be if she messed up.

Two wrongs didn't make a right. And she didn't want to be the kind of person who had to punish someone else for their sin against her. She wanted to be the kind of person who left that in God's hands, and loved and forgave people anyway. Especially her husband.

As they walked toward the garden, where a group of people were gathering already, she closed her eyes and breathed in deeply.

"It's beautiful, even out here. Just looking at it."

"That arch was a work of art. I'm glad you thought of it."

"I'm glad you could take my design and make it. Even though you're not a welder, as you said multiple times."

"I'm not a welder by trade, but I did learn a lot more than what I already knew making that gate. I... That's probably one of my favorite things I've ever made."

"Yeah, this is probably one of my favorite gardens. Although, I'm very partial to the one that we just put together in Raspberry Ridge. I'm curious to see how it will look in a few years from now when the plants grow up a little, and everything is blooming on schedule."

"I think it will be our crowning glory. Even if it doesn't have an arch and a gate."

"It's going to have a fence, and most likely a gate, just nothing this fancy."

"Sometimes fancy isn't better, but this fancy works."

Pittsburgh was a steel city, and the rustic, iron gate fit in with the blue-collar, hardworking ethic that was reminiscent of the founding of Pittsburgh.

Something light and breezy would have been completely off place, and Vera had known that the first day she started touring the city to get an eye for what she was going to design.

It had to be something substantial, something tough and strong, something tough as steel. And yet something that healed, something that soothed the soul, something that represented the past and yet brought hope for the future.

She thought they had been successful.

As more and more people gathered, she thought that maybe this would be the biggest turnout they'd ever had at one of their celebrations, although they had all been grand openings. Maybe people had a tendency to show up more at ten-year anniversaries. She had nothing on which to base it.

"Dominic! Well, my goodness, I've been looking for you everywhere, and you've been hiding over here."

Vera recognized Shoshana from her image online. She zeroed in on Dominic, with her arms out, going in for a hug.

Because Dominic never let go of her hand, she could feel how he stiffened, how he drew back a bit, how he stopped himself from cringing back and allowed the woman to throw her arms around him.

He pulled back before Shoshana did and took a step back and closer to Vera, pulling his hand out of hers in order to put his arm around her shoulders.

"I don't think you've met my wife, Vera. Vera, this is Shoshana."

"Vera, thank you so much for allowing me to borrow your husband. He's a genius at building my designs and infusing them with life and flair. Of all the designs I've done, the one he and I did is my very favorite. He just has such a way of reaching into my brain and doing exactly what I think." She had admiration in her eyes and wiggled them at Dominic in a way that sent slime crawling up Vera's backbone. "I've never met anyone who can read my mind and bring my designs to life the way he can."

"We worked together one time, so technically, it's design, not designs."

Dominic was not usually technical, and he didn't typically split hairs, so that was a little odd coming from him at that point, and Vera wasn't quite sure why he insisted on saying it. On making the distinction.

"But we're soon to be working on another," Shoshana said, and then she gave a little squeal. "I'm so excited! I can't wait to talk about it today. I am going to announce it from the podium. And I even have some slides to show everyone and a handout for the local news outlets of the designs I have already ready. It is an honor to be able to design for Hollywood, and this is going to send our careers into the stratosphere," she said, acting like that was the best thing that could ever happen to them, to have their career shoot into the stratosphere.

But maybe one thing Vera learned from the death of her son was that it didn't matter if her career shot into the stratosphere. If she didn't have her family behind her, their support, their love and care, that meant more than anything, and she would rather not have a stratospheric career, if it meant she'd lose her family.

"Dominic Miller! I love your work, and your design with Shoshana is my absolute favorite ever!" A perky blonde hopped over, giving Shoshana a squeeze before shaking Dominic's hand.

Vera thought about Jesus. She wanted to turn her eyes on Jesus and allow the things of the world to fade away, like the pain of hearing that the one design her husband had built with someone else was someone's favorite of all his work, including the many designs he'd done with her and the one they were celebrating today. Even if the person who said it was obviously a friend of Shoshana's.

She swallowed and tried to be happy for Shoshana and her husband as the blonde continued to gush about how Dominic and Shoshana made an incredible team. She was going to have to get used to this. Dominic could not take back the work he had done, and this would follow Vera until the day she died. How sad to live her life, unhappy and hurt anytime someone loved Shoshana's work with Dominic more than hers. She would not allow herself to live like that.

"Shoshana, I see you found the main squeeze," a burly, bearded man said, coming over, putting an arm around Shoshana, and giving her a little hug before reaching out the same arm and offering it to Dominic. "I'm Todd Vander, president of the Pittsburgh council. It's good to finally meet you."

Dominic shook the proffered hand. "It's great to be back in Pittsburgh."

"The mayor will be here shortly. I'm so glad you and your lovely wife could make it," he said, offering his hand to Vera. She liked a man who wasn't afraid to shake her hand, and didn't spend all of his time talking to just her husband, but shifted his eyes between both of them.

Dominic looked uncomfortable, like he had wanted to say something as a rebuttal to Shoshana, but Todd coming up had precluded him being able to say anything, unless he wanted all the details of their conversation to be public.

Still, his arm was still around Vera, and she allowed him to hold her close.

At least he was signaling who he wanted. And it wasn't Shoshana, since he had stepped away from her and stepped toward Vera.

It made her feel much better that Dominic was not going to allow Shoshana to pull him away from her.

She needed him by her side anyway. Even if he was the one who had caused the pain in her chest to begin with. He hadn't done it on purpose, of that she was sure.

Thirty-One

Dominic and Vera chatted with Todd for a while as some other council members made their way over, and folks continued to chat.

Shoshana stayed near Dominic the entire time. Almost as though she was afraid to leave him, that he might do something without her knowledge or run away from her.

It was interesting to Vera that Todd, member of the Pittsburgh city council, who knew Shoshana well enough to put a casual arm around her shoulders, had hired them to do this project, but maybe he had just recently heard of Shoshana, since the woman didn't seem to be shy about inserting herself into anything. Maybe Todd had met Shoshana through Dominic. Perhaps he would want Dominic and Shoshana to do Pittsburgh's next project.

Vera shoved that thought away. And she couldn't blame Shoshana for trying to tie herself to anyone to get ahead. If she was concerned about her career and attaining stratospheric status, that's what she needed to do—get pushed up by Vera's work, team up with her husband, and rub shoulders with people who controlled contracts and money.

"I just wanted to thank you for the garden. It was a great comfort to me when my twins died at Pittsburgh Children's. They... They were conjoined, and neither one of them made it." A woman put her hand on her arm and talked to Vera, tears gathering in the woman's eyes as she relayed how the healing garden had helped her through that hard time.

"I lost a child of my own, he was a little older, eight, but it was the most heartbreaking thing that had ever happened to me," she said, and her heartbreak automatically gave her a connection to that woman she wouldn't have had without Trent's passing.

She found that over and over as she spoke with folks who had gathered for the celebration.

She hadn't been able to talk of Trent before. Since his death, this was the first time that she had gone to one of her gardens and actually spoken of her loss. But she could see that immediately people related to her, understood the pain, felt it too, whether they had lost a son or daughter or sister or a parent or grandparent, or even a spouse. Like Mrs. Bomar, whom Vera saw shortly before the ceremony was to begin. They all had lost someone, and as soon as they knew that Vera, too, had suffered a great loss, it was like there was a bond between them that gave them something in common that nothing else could.

Until a person had lost someone close to them, they couldn't understand the grief and sorrow and pain that a human went through during loss.

"No wonder you design such beautiful gardens, having experienced pain yourself," another woman said as they spoke.

Vera shook her head. "When I designed this garden, I hadn't gone through that. But now that I have, I understand the need a lot better. And I understand why it's necessary,"

"Your insight is inspiring. I've often wondered about the person who designed this, even wondering about the person who built it. Did they know? Had they felt the pain? Did they understand what was happening to me?" The woman shook her head. "It'll be even better to know that you felt the pain of loss as well. I think there's something in human nature that, while I wouldn't wish anything terrible on anyone, it makes me feel better to know that I'm not alone in my experience."

"Ladies and gentlemen, gather around, we're getting ready to start."

Vera squeezed the woman's hand in sympathy. "Excuse me, my

husband and I need to go to the front, but maybe we can chat some more later."

"I just appreciate some of your time. It was great to meet you. Thanks for making a trip today. I know it helped me, and I bet it'll help a lot of others. I'm getting it for my social media," the lady said, holding up her phone.

"Wow. Okay. Thanks."

Vera knew that people often took pictures and posted them online, but to know someone personally who had suffered loss, and found healing in her design and in Dominic's construction, and was going to be talking about that online, put everything in a different perspective.

"Oh, let me come with you guys. I think I speak right before you do."

Shoshana hurried along, grabbing a hold of Dominic's arm and pressing herself against his side.

His arm had come out from around Vera's shoulders, but he kept tight hold of her hand.

When they reached the steps, he pulled away from Shoshana and put a hand on the rail so Vera and he could ascend the steps together.

There were no assigned seats on the makeshift platform, but Todd indicated they should sit in the chairs that had been provided alongside.

"I'll give the opening remarks, then the mayor is going to speak, then Shoshana is going to speak—she requested to do so—and the council gave her permission. And then Dominic, and then Vera. Then we'll have the mayor say a few closing words."

"All right, that sounds good," Vera said as Dominic steered her toward the second chair and had her sit, then he took the seat beside her on the edge, so Shoshana had no choice but to sit beside Vera.

Vera wanted to ignore her, turn her back to her, and strike up a conversation with her husband, but...she remembered the Bible verse that commanded something different, and she whispered it to herself. Love your enemies, bless them that curse you, do good to them that hate you, and pray for them which despitefully use you, and persecute you.

Lord, I can't do this in my human frailty, but I can do it with Your power. I need You.

She turned to Shoshana. "How long have you and Dominic known each other?" She hadn't even considered how they had met. Whether Dominic had bid on the job of hers, or whether she had requested him as a builder.

"Well, technically, we just met in person for the first time today. But we've talked a lot online. Every day at some point. After all, the design we did together was rather complicated."

Vera nodded her head, thinking that was probably a slam against her designs, which Shoshana obviously thought were simple. Regardless, rather than give some rebuttal about her and Dominic working very closely and speaking every day, she just nodded.

"Well, that's nice that you two finally got to meet."

"Yes. I've been dying to meet him. He's left a meeting where I've just missed him several times, and we just missed each other on the job a couple of times as well. But as fate would have it, we're here today together."

"Sure," Vera said. And Shoshana launched into a long soliloquy about her and Dominic and how wonderful their design was. Listening to her talk was like listening to someone who was only interested in themselves, since she spoke like Dominic and she were the only ones on the platform.

"I knew he would be honored to work with me when I sent my first request to him. He practically jumped on it, I mean, it wasn't even a day before he answered me back. It was obvious he was eager. I do know that I have somewhat of a reputation, and if you've noticed in the last issue of *Design America*, I was listed as the number one designer in the country. It was quite a coup for him to be able to get my interest and to design with me. I do believe that we will be designing many things in the future together, won't we, Dominic?" Shoshana said, leaning over Vera and trying to draw Dominic into the conversation.

His gaze was focused over the crowd, and he didn't look toward her until she said his name again.

"I'm sorry?" he said.

"We're going to be working a lot more together, right?" she said, almost as though she were demanding that he agree with her immediately, right there and then.

"Actually, I made a decision not that long ago that... I know that it's kind of weird, that I wouldn't want my career to be the most important thing in my life, and that there's plenty of opportunity for growth and I'm maybe not taking it, but my decision was that if I work again, it's only going to be with my wife."

Vera turned her head to look fully at him. "You mean that?"

"I do. I want to talk to you, but we had so much going on lately, and things are so...busy, it just never seems like a good time to start a conversation that might not have the best results or have us leave feeling good about each other. But maybe tonight?"

She nodded. He had the same issues she had, and it made her feel a little bit...weird to know that he had things he wanted to talk to her about but had put them off, like there was something hard about talking to her.

But she couldn't get upset or offended, because she had done the exact same thing to him. And for no reason. There wasn't anything difficult about talking to Dominic, but just for the reason that he had said—that she didn't want them to have a hard conversation sometime when they were doing something and she didn't want him to be upset or...it just never seemed like a good time.

"I understand." She nodded. "I felt the same way."

He narrowed his eyes, like he was wondering what she might be talking about.

"We'll get it all hashed out. I'm sure we will," she said, and the assurance that she felt must have shown on her face.

Because he nodded and said, "I'm sure we will too."

The hymn ran through her mind again, *and the things of earth will grow strangely dim, in the light of His glory and grace.*

Then Todd got up and began thanking people for coming, explaining what they were there for, and talking a little bit about how the healing garden had helped people over the years. Some of the stories he told made Vera want to cry. She had no idea that her garden had done so much good.

He introduced Shoshana, and she walked up to the microphone.

It wasn't a surprise to Vera when she thanked everyone for coming, acted like she belonged there, and announced that she would be doing a design with Dominic, the builder of this design, out in California.

Vera actually felt a little bad for her, even though she looked great, in a bright pink pantsuit, her blonde hair flowing down past her shoulders, her voice perky and excited.

But the people who came here today didn't care about a design in California. They didn't care about Shoshana designing it. They wanted to know about themselves, their city, their needs.

Vera saw that clearly as Shoshana spoke, pushing herself and her agenda and not really giving a thought to the people she was talking to.

There was lukewarm applause as Shoshana stopped and walked triumphantly back to her seat.

Maybe the smile that she gave Vera and Dominic was a superior smile, almost as though she had made it official, and now he would look ridiculous if he disputed her claim.

But Dominic didn't even mention Shoshana or his next project when he stood up to the microphone.

He said, "When I built this healing garden, I didn't know that it wasn't going to be long before I needed a healing garden of my own."

The crowd had gone completely silent.

"My wife and I lost our son a year and a half ago, and it was the hardest loss I'd ever endured. It wasn't until she suggested, not that long ago, that we make a healing garden in our hometown of Raspberry Ridge that it actually occurred to me that maybe what I had been doing for a living would help me as a person.

"I like to stay busy. I don't want to sit around and think about things. I like to keep my hands going. My wife is more of a thinker. She ponders things. I don't know how the designs come to her. Maybe you can find out when she comes up here to speak." There was a ripple of laughter.

"But I suppose that my emotions come out through these." He held up his hands. "Like I said, when I built this garden, I didn't know the hard sting of grief, but I can tell you that I built it with love. I built it with the city of Pittsburgh in mind. I built it thinking of my wife, and how much I love working with her, and how much her designs mean to me, how they speak to my heart, and how every nail, every board, every piece of dirt that I put down, I pray we just bring her designs to life in the way that she meant it, so that it will be a blessing to others, because she designed it with you all in mind. And I was just the one who was honored and privileged enough to be allowed to take her design and put concrete things behind it. Thank you for allowing us to be here in Pittsburgh, and a huge thank you to my wife, for the design, for the privilege of being able to work with her, and for the even greater privilege of being married to her. There is no greater honor."

He nodded his head, and then he went back and sat down at his seat, somehow avoiding Vera's eyes.

She did not know how she was supposed to get up and speak after he had just said all of those things about her.

He wouldn't look at her, but he did lean over and whisper in her ear as Todd got back up, still clapping, along with everyone else, to introduce her.

"You're going to do great," he said.

"We'll talk about what you just said later," she said to him. She didn't have enough time to tell him what she thought about his speech now. He should have warned her he was going to say something that was going to make her cry.

How was she supposed to talk now?

"And now the designer of our garden, who has honored us with her presence today, and we're eager to hear what she has to say. Please welcome Vera Miller," Todd said.

There was applause as she stood up, leaving her husband's side, walking over to the podium.

She waited for the applause to die down and prayed she would say the things God wanted her to.

"I had the privilege of talking to some of you beforehand, and I'm guessing there are more stories like the ones that Todd spoke of when he was introducing us. And that's the reason I do this. God gave me a gift, and He wanted me to use it to bring honor and glory to Him. I know sometimes I go off the rails a little, like every other human on the planet." There was a ripple of laughter.

"But that's what I want with my life. I want it to point everyone to Jesus. And Jesus is the great physician. He's the one who heals the heartbreak, the loneliness and despair, the depth of sadness that we can't possibly know until we lose someone who means almost everything to us. And then somehow we're expected to continue on without them. I suppose that's what the purpose of this garden is, a place of quiet contemplation as we enjoy the beauty of God's creation, so we can figure out how our hearts can be healed from such grievous heartbreak and pain, and how we can be closer to our Savior, through that experience."

There wasn't a sound other than the gentle blowing of the wind and a soft trickle of water, and she took a breath and then said, "That's my prayer for this garden. That the earthly things will fade, and that Jesus will come into focus as we sit here in contemplation. And if there's anything good in the design of the garden, it's because Jesus took my humble thoughts, gave me a husband who is amazing, and blessed the outcome. I hope this garden is enjoyed for many years to come."

The entire place erupted in cheers and applause as she finished her speech, gave a small wave to the crowd, and walked back to her seat.

The applause continued unabated for a long time, until her husband, still clapping, leaned over and said, "That was the best speech I ever heard." He continued to clap, and then he added, "Especially the part about how wonderful your husband is. You might have to say that part again later for me, just so I can make sure I heard it right."

She gave him a gentle nudge with her shoulder and then turned her head and kissed his cheek.

His hands stopped mid clap, and his eyes turned to hers, then he started clapping again, louder than ever.

Thirty-Two

T he celebration had taken longer than they thought, and then they stopped at a small café and grabbed a bite to eat.

The sun was setting as they pulled into their Airbnb.

"What a day," Dominic said as he put the car in park and shut it off.

"It turned out a little differently than what I was expecting," Vera said, thinking about all of the things that had shifted for her today.

Instead of seeing Shoshana as a rival, she saw her as someone to be kind to. Because she didn't have what Vera had, not nearly, and she desperately wanted and was chasing after something that was not going to make her happy.

That, and Vera had realized how much her work had comforted grieving people just like her. If she had had a prayer garden, maybe she would have spent time at that, rather than as much time at Trent's grave.

She didn't know, but she did appreciate the fact that now she had one of her own and hadn't realized how essential they could be in a person's life.

"All right, let's go see these fancy digs we've got for tonight," Dominic said, grabbing his door handle and yanking open his door.

He opened the trunk and grabbed both bags, closing it and coming around the front.

"I think the door code is in the email," he said as they walked around the house, looking for the door with a lock on it.

"Yeah, I have it up. I was just waiting on you," Vera said, saying the number to him so he could punch it into the keypad.

The lock swished, and Dominic opened the door, allowing her to walk in first while he came in carrying the luggage.

She adjusted her purse strap over her shoulder and gazed in awe at the floor-to-ceiling windows and the amazing view of the city of Pittsburgh.

"I guess I should take my shoes off," she said, stopping to kick her shoes off and smothering her sigh of relief.

She always wore comfortable shoes, but even comfortable shoes felt good when they came off.

"Wow. That is quite a view," Dominic said, rolling the bags as far as the hall and then joining her at the edge of the living room. It was all one great room, with the kitchen to the right as a person walked in, a closet or something to the left, along with a bench and an area for coats and shoes. A hall went off to the left, and the great room stretched out in front of them, huge cathedral ceilings, with windows the whole way to the top.

"Glad I'm not afraid of heights," Vera said as she walked forward slowly, looking at the Pittsburgh skyline and then her gaze dipping down, to the river at the bottom of what looked like a cliff.

"Is the house built on a cliff?" she asked, turning to Dominic.

"Yeah, I think it might be. You couldn't really tell that from the pictures, but it definitely looks that way from here."

"I think there was another really nice view in the bedroom," Vera said. "But I don't want to go check, because the sunset is just getting good."

Dominic had toed his shoes off as well and now sat down on the couch. "I think I'll enjoy it from here, unless you had somewhere else you wanted to go?"

"No. That looks good," she said, glancing back to where he sat on the couch and making a decision to go and sit beside him, but on the end, leaving a few inches between them.

Back before Trent's death, she would have cuddled up next to him, but they were going to be talking, at least she hoped they were, and she thought that maybe having a little bit of space between them might be a good idea.

They sat in silence for a while, just enjoying the beauty of the sunset. Her stomach felt content from their recent meal, and so did she.

"I hadn't realized until today how much the work that you and I have done has impacted people for good. Sometimes I wonder what I'm going to do with my life, what I'm going to leave behind, you know? How people are going to hell and wondering what I can do to make the world a little better place, how I can encourage people. I feel like I need to go do something, and I didn't realize I was already doing something."

"I had a sneaking suspicion about it, to be honest, but today really was an eye-opener for me as well. To hear the stories of the people who had lost so much and found so much peace in something that you and I had made. It made me...feel like our marriage itself was a blessing to people. The fact that you and I love each other, spend our lives together, and work together was a blessing. You know?"

She hadn't thought of that at all, and that was one of the things about being with Dominic, he always showed her a different perspective, and she loved that.

She looked back out over the sunset. It was at its pinnacle, with bright, brilliant hues of orange and pink giving way to deeper blues as the sun slowly sank down.

It all reflected off the river below them. She thought it might have been the Ohio, but Pittsburgh was so twisted and convoluted, she kind of lost her sense of direction and wasn't sure which river they crossed, since they crossed about three bridges on their way here.

Finally, as the sunset started to fade, she decided she wasn't going to put off what she wanted to talk about any longer.

"When I got on our scheduling website, to see what your schedule was, I looked to see who had permission to view and edit the schedule. Shoshana's name was on there. It...gave me pause, because you'd never said anything to me about adding her, and...if you've only worked with her once, I didn't understand why she needed to be there."

She thought that that sounded pretty good, not accusatory, and not angry. Her voice was modulated and calm, and she lifted her brows in question.

Part of her calmness, she had to admit, came from her conversation with Shoshana, when she had said that it was the first time she and Dominic had met in person.

She didn't know whether Shoshana was normally an honest person, or whether she was prone to lying, but unless she was deliberately trying to hide something, it eased Vera's mind that she had said it.

"I forgot she was on there, to be honest," Dominic said, and she believed him immediately.

She lifted her chin, trying to push back the hurt. Just the fact that he admitted putting her on felt...painful. That was her scheduling place with her husband, not her husband and some other woman. And then, there was the whole can of worms that he worked with her, and all that other stuff that she had been trying so hard to put behind her.

Turn your eyes upon Jesus, look full in His wonderful face, and the things of earth will grow strangely dim, in the light of His glory and grace.

She tried to think about Jesus, think about his glory, his majesty and power, and how he had given it all up to come to earth, to make the sacrifice to be the salvation of the world, and no one appreciated it.

They crucified him instead.

She crucified him.

Because it was her sin he was dying for. And she wouldn't have been any different than anybody else in those times. She would have done the same thing. She would have been right there, wanting him crucified, and yet he was doing it for her. Had done it for her.

Whatever thing her husband had done that had hurt her was nothing compared to what Jesus had given for her. What he'd forgiven her from. What he'd sacrificed for her. That's why she needed to keep her eyes on him.

"Is that what you wanted to talk to me about?" Dominic said, after she didn't say anything.

"Yeah. Mostly. She calls you a lot, and...you worked with her."

She wasn't going to get upset about it. She was going to be calm, but she didn't look at her husband. She kept her eyes on the fading sky, and while she didn't intend it to, her voice sounded...depressed. "I thought it was just you and me. And...that hurt."

She didn't want to admit that. Admit the weakness, admit that he had done something that had been so painful to her, something she struggled so hard to get over. He would never know how hard and painful it had been for her. Hopefully, if she could keep her mouth shut and her eyes on Jesus.

"I'm sorry," he said immediately. "I really am." He reached out to touch her, and she allowed it, but she looked at his hand and then looked away.

He removed it.

She had to admit she felt grateful. She didn't want to be touched right now. Not by someone who had hurt her so much. She loved their tender, touching moments. The little things they did to be a blessing to each other, the little touches they shared. She loved cuddling and rubbing her husband's back, threading her fingers through his hair, feeling him do the same to her, but not right now. She felt...vulnerable, and now that she'd admitted that he hurt her, she...had to admit that she hoped for an apology. An explanation. A confession that he was wrong. That he wouldn't do it again.

She didn't deserve it necessarily, because she was created to serve others, and bring glory to God, not to get what she deserved. But she wanted it.

"I... One of the biggest mistakes in my life was to accept her proposal when she contacted me and asked me to work with her. I really don't have any excuses, other than it was shortly after Trent died, and you were curled up on your side of the bed, getting up before me, staying away, and I needed to be busy. And yeah, I could have been busy around the house. I wish I would have made those flower boxes, and put in the flower garden, and all those other things that we were planning on doing. That would have kept me busy, but so much of that revolved around Trent. Trent's playset, Trent's sandbox, Trent's basketball hoop, all the designs that you made had Trent right in the middle of them, and I couldn't stand it."

He fell silent.

"I'm sorry I turned away from you. You're right about that. And I figured that that was probably why you accepted Shoshana's proposal. Because... I wasn't there. I was deep in my own grief, wrapped up in my head, trying to process it, and wasn't helping you at all. I'm sorry about that. That was my mistake."

"I'm sorry. I kind of blamed everything on you just now, and that wasn't what I meant to do. I made a mistake. I accepted Shoshana's proposal, and I should not have. I could have done anything else to stay busy. I didn't have to accept the proposal from your competitor, although... I justified it a little bit by saying to myself that me working with her would bring attention to you."

He paused, and she didn't move. Why in the world would he have thought that? She supposed she could see that perhaps Shoshana's fans would be introduced to her designs. But Shoshana's designs were so much different than hers that if someone liked Shoshana's things, they probably weren't going to like her things as well.

She didn't want to explain that to her husband.

"That wasn't why I accepted in the first place, but I justified it to myself afterward that perhaps it would help you make a name for yourself, to be linked with me, and I was linked with her. I...guess I tried to tell myself I was actually helping you, when in reality, I was just being selfish."

He blew out a breath. "I could see that a little today when she was around us. She was trying to push you aside. And I'm sorry. I can't undo it. I wish I could. I hate that there is a design out there that I worked on and built, that has my name linked with hers. I'm sure it probably irritates you every time you see it."

That was for sure.

"I can look away. Maybe it's a blessing to people."

That wasn't what she wanted to say, but it was what she had to say. He couldn't undo it. Couldn't undo what he had done. It was there. And she supposed that was the way sin was, although she didn't necessarily look at this as sin, it just...left a mark. When someone made a mistake, made a poor decision, the fallout would always be there. Hurting.

She had to figure out how to give it to God and allow Him to work it however He wanted to. If He wanted to make the project that they completed together be better than any of the projects that she and her husband did together, then she supposed it was up to the Lord.

"Vera, I wasn't thinking of you. I suspected before you said something, but it's obvious now what I did hurt you, pretty deeply. And I never intended for it to. I just...made a stupid, foolish decision. Partly because I wanted to stay busy, and partly because I thought it would be good for my career, maybe that was bigger than anything. Because I was selfish, I thought working with two top designers would be better than working with just one. I... And maybe it would have been. Maybe if my career was the most important thing, it would have been a good decision, but my career is not more important than you are. Also, it was easy to see that Shoshana does not have the character you do, and as soon as someone else comes along that she thinks is better than me, she'll leave without a backward glance. You, on the other hand, will stand beside me forever."

Thirty-Three

Dominic's words were like a balm to Vera's soul. They soothed something that had been bothering her for a long time, something that had hurt and caused her to pull away even more than what she already had.

"I'm sorry, I should have said something before."

"If you had, I would have canceled things with her. I... I don't want you to think that anything that I did with her was more important than you. I know my actions didn't show that, but if you give me another chance, I meant what I said today. I've been thinking about it a lot, and working with you, my wife, my life partner, my soulmate, is better than a billion dollars and all the accolades in the world. I don't want to take another design project that you aren't working with me on. A few houses here and there or something, unless you have a problem with that, if we needed to make ends meet, but I have enough money. What I want is you." He paused, and then as though he were afraid of her reaction, he said, "And whatever family God gives us."

Her eyes widened, and while his words had made her feel amazing, warm and soft and sweet on the inside, his last statement shocked her.

But through her newfound lens, she realized that it was selfish of her to refuse to even try.

"All right. Whatever family God gives us. And thank you for everything else. I honestly was worried that there was something more going on between you and Shoshana."

"No!" He shook his head. "I feel guilty for accepting her offer, and then I didn't want to be unkind to her or offend her in any way because I didn't know whether you being associated with her through me would help your career at all. That's the only reason I hadn't shut her down completely about the next project. I, believe it or not, was thinking of you. Obviously, I was wrong, and it would have been kinder for me to just tell her I wasn't interested, rather than making you wonder if there was something going on."

"I couldn't figure out why she kept calling you. And then when I saw that you had added her to the calendar site..."

"About that. She kept bugging me. When are you going to start? When are you going to be done? How soon are you going to be done with your last project? Stuff like that, daily, and you know what I do. I'm outside working all day. I don't have time to answer her fifteen texts or emails or whatever. So I just added her on and then told her she could check that anytime she needed to remember what I said." He lifted his shoulder. "I honestly forgot I did it. But I'll take her off as soon as we get home. I don't want her on there. It was just...easier to have her there than to be constantly dealing with her."

Relief washed through Vera. And she was so very, very thankful that she hadn't jumped to the wrong conclusion. It would have been an easy thing to do, but his explanation made perfect sense. And she felt bad for him, for having to deal with that.

But she could see how her turning away to begin with had started everything in motion. Not that it justified what Dominic had done. She did not think that it did, but she did understand it better now.

"I was always afraid that if we tried to have children, I would be watching every month to see, and I would be deeply disappointed every month that went by that I didn't have a child, and... I think my whole life would get wrapped up in that, and I'm scared. Because that would be painful. Maybe more painful than I want to go through. I... I feel like I've already gone through the pain of losing Trent. I don't want to go through the pain of every month knowing that God didn't bless me again. And then wondering what's wrong with me, why I'm not getting the one thing that I want, and why people who have children and don't want them... All the women who are going for abortions every day, and here I am, begging God to give me a child, and I don't get one."

He stared at her, like he had never thought of any of that before. And she realized she really hadn't shared it. It was just those deep, dark things that were in a woman's heart and typically didn't see the light of day.

"We don't have to. We can just assume that our family is done. And whatever God gives us, He gives us."

"Well, He didn't give us even one more for the eight years Trent was alive."

"I know," he said, and his voice cracked, and she felt so bad for him that she leaned to the side and put a hand on his arm. He allowed it to slide down and linked their fingers together.

"I've been working on a new mindset. Something had to give, because the way I was after Trent's death wasn't working very well."

"I appreciate that." He sounded sincere and not sarcastic, which she appreciated.

"You're too good to me. I deserve a lot more flak from you for the way I just pulled into myself."

"I know that's the way you handle things. When you get a blow like that, you get quiet, go off alone, kind of like a hurt dog. They go underneath the porch and just lick their wounds. I know that's what you do."

"I think you just called me a dog. But everything else was very considerate of you."

He laughed. "We already established the fact that I wasn't very considerate and what I did was a lot worse. At least you just went off by yourself. I... I didn't cheat on you, not in this lifetime, that will never happen. But...I know I hurt you."

"I really appreciate you not saying 'okay, I apologized once, and let's just forget it now, okay?'" She laughed a little. "It just helps me to hear every once in a while that you're sorry, because every once in a while, it hurts."

"I'll try to remember then."

"I don't want to keep throwing anything up into your face. Because like I said, I made mistakes, I did things wrong, this is not all you, this is...actually, my fault to begin with, since I started it."

"I'm not allowing you to keep me from taking the blame. You should be able to do whatever you want to do, and I should still be your faithful, protective, caring, absolutely devoted husband. That's what I want. No matter what you do."

"Yeah. That was something else I was thinking, that no matter what went on with you and Shoshana, and I didn't know. All these worst-case scenarios were in my brain, and I would have to think, it doesn't matter, I love you. I pledged to love you, and that has to look a certain way. You know? Through thick or thin, hard times, and easy times. I can't just... be a good wife when things are going easy. Right?"

He nodded. "And it's the other side of the coin that applies to me."

The sunlight had faded, but it wasn't completely dark, because of the lights of the city shining through the window as they sat on the couch, their hands linked, sharing their hearts and forgiving and loving. The lights cast a glow that was almost romantic. Kind of like moonlight in the country.

"Dance with me," he said softly.

"There's no music." She laughed, even as she started standing up.

"I can sing something, or let me get something up on my phone."

"I love hearing you sing, but real music is nice too."

He didn't say anything more, but pulled up a slow, romantic song on his phone, and set it on the coffee table, grabbing her hands and pulling her around, so they were standing in front of the window. He put his arms around her, drawing her close, and she laid her head on his chest, wrapping her arms around him, as their bodies moved slowly together. Familiar and right.

"I missed this. Missed you. I understand where you were and what you were doing, but I missed you."

"I hope we don't ever go through anything like that again, but I can promise you if we do, I will try as hard as I can not to disappear on you again."

"Whatever you have to do to heal this." He pointed to her heart and then put his hand on her temple, pushing her hair back away from her face, as she lifted her head and looked up at him.

"It's not just about me. Let me be considerate of you too. Don't give me a free pass."

"You have a free pass for the rest of your life. And the reason I can say that is because I know that you're not going to take advantage of it. You... You always treat me better than you treat yourself. You've inspired me to try to be the same. I don't want to be the same though, with every woman I meet. I want to make sure it's special for us. Otherwise, what's the point in us being together?"

"Same."

"And I've never once looked at you and another man and thought that you were anything but kindly polite. Never once."

"You know what, there are benefits to being married to a man who is so honest, you know he couldn't possibly tell a lie, even if he wanted to."

"You know, pride goes before a fall, and don't ever think that someone can't sin, but lying is one of those things that I hate with all my heart."

They continued to sway to music, and his hand ran down her hair, down her back, sending shivers the whole way down.

"I prayed that we would be able to get through this and that our relationship would be stronger than it was before. Because there was a time when I came out of my funk that I wondered if the gulf between us wasn't so wide that it couldn't be bridged."

"You sent me an email that had the word divorce in it, and that shook me to my bones. I don't even think that word. It's not in my vocabulary. I'm with you until I die. And you're stuck with me, unless you go through an awful lot of trouble to get unstuck."

"I decided before I came today, no matter what happened, no matter what you said, no matter what went on with Shoshana, I loved you. I loved you then, I love you now, and I promised and vowed to love you. How can I walk away from all the promises I made, just because you possibly made a mistake?"

"I think that's my free pass for the rest of my life."

"And I can give that to you, because I know the kind of man you are and I trust you. I had a really hard time believing that you might have cheated on me, despite all the evidence mounting up against you. It just didn't make sense. Except... There had been such a rift between us."

"So let's not let that happen again."

"Yeah."

His lips came down and touched her temple. He kept them there, and she closed her eyes and felt from his gentle touch how much he loved her.

"Can I ask you another hard question?" he finally asked, softly, sounding a little strange, like he didn't want to.

"Sure."

They just decided that there wasn't anything that was going to come between them, so she braced herself but knew that she would face this, with her new thoughts, that she would keep her eyes on Jesus, that she would try to make sure that she responded correctly, so that God got the glory, and not allow her pride or the thought that she deserved anything to get in the way.

"Is there a reason that you've been sleeping on your side of the bed, curled up in a ball, as far from me as you can get?"

Of course he would ask her that question directly, no hinting, no carefully approaching it from a vague perspective. No, he would tell her the way it was, which was exactly what she wanted.

"I guess...at first it was because of Trent, and what I was dealing with, and then it was because of you working with Shoshana. It hurt, and...I didn't want to be intimate with someone who was hurting me so much. I just... I didn't think I could do it."

She took a breath, knowing that her words weren't easy and she was bringing up what they had just buried, but she didn't want to not tell him, since he had asked.

"But I think I'm okay."

"Are you sure?" he asked, his lips pressing against her head, then down her cheek, to the edge of her jaw.

She lifted her head and put their cheeks together. "Yeah. I'm sure."

Maybe he turned his head first, or maybe she did, or maybe, from the decade plus that they spent together, they did it at the same time, instinctively, but their heads turned, and their mouths met, and the chasm that she had imagined between them disappeared, as a figment of her imagination, like it had never been there to begin with. And maybe it hadn't. Maybe it had been something that she had constructed, out of fear and a lack of faith and an unwillingness to take the first step.

The kiss was soft and gentle at first, an apology maybe, a tentative step in the direction they both wanted to take, testing whether the other was ready.

But it deepened at some point, and she found herself clinging to her husband, breathless and with weak knees, holding on for dear life.

"I love you. I never stopped, but I haven't said it in a while, I'm sorry. I love you more than life."

She smiled. She believed him. "You too. So much." More than herself. Maybe that was one good thing that she had found out through this all, that she was willing to give up herself to prove her love or to show her love for her husband.

It was a good thing their plane didn't leave until after noon the next day, since they were up for a good while after that. They did get to see the view of the city from the bedroom. Although neither of them spent much time looking at it. Not for a while anyway.

Join Jessie's list and be the first to know about new releases and sales on her books!

Read Under the Rising Moon, the next book in the Raspberry Ridge series. Homer finds someone unexpected in his garage and his life will never be the same. Opposites attract, all the beach vibes and see more of your favorite characters from Raspberry Ridge. Keep reading for a sneak peek now.

Sneak Peek of Under the Rising Moon

"Please stop."

Skyler Montgomery held one hand over her protruding belly, massaging the spot on the top left that always seemed to ache. Maybe the baby's head was pushing against her skin there.

"We just stopped. What's wrong with you?" Jeff Lewis, her boyfriend, er, fiancé, and the father of her baby, gave her a derisive look.

She felt like she was really putting him out by asking him to stop. "I'm pregnant. That's what's wrong. Your child is sitting on my bladder."

She tried to keep her voice modulated and not sound as annoyed as she felt. It wasn't her fault she had to pee. Was she supposed to pretend that she didn't? Suffer in silence? It wasn't like she demanded that he stop. She'd asked nicely.

The exit flew by, and she gritted her teeth.

"I really need to go. You're going to have to stop at the next exit, or you're going to have a mess on your nice pickup seat to clean up."

It wasn't an idle threat. She felt like she couldn't wait any longer. She'd tried to wait as long as she could before she said something, because she knew his reaction was going to be the way it was. That's the way it had been the last three times she'd asked to stop.

It wasn't like she was going every fifteen minutes. It had been two hours since they stopped before.

"You're more of a pain in the butt than you're worth," he mumbled to himself. "If you pee on my pickup seat, you're going to regret it."

He'd never exactly threatened her, but there were times, like now, that he made her feel like his possessions were more important than she was.

"Please. Let's don't fight. This is our last time together as a couple before the baby comes."

She was due in two weeks. And she had felt like she and Jeff were drifting apart. She knew she shouldn't have slept with him to begin with, not without a ring, a golden band, not the tiny engagement stone he'd given her, even if it had been a bit snug and she no longer wore it because her fingers had swelled with her pregnancy. But he'd been very persuasive, and she hadn't wanted him to get mad at her.

Plus, an engagement was almost like being married. They were committed to each other. There was nothing that could break their bond.

Anyway, she felt like they were drifting apart and had asked him to take a long weekend to spend it with her. She wanted to renew their spark because when the baby arrived, she'd been told that she'd be very busy, and sometimes relationships suffered in the newborn stage.

Hopefully her baby would be a good one, would sleep through the night, and would hardly ever cry.

It would be the first thing in her life that was easy, but she kinda felt like God owed her something easy, after all the hard things she'd gone through. She could hear her grandma saying that God didn't owe anyone anything, but she pushed those thoughts aside and set her jaw stubbornly. She could also hear her gram saying that she was too stubborn for her own good, then her Aunt Ruth, Gram's sister, would say, "Oh, Roberta, she's determined. She has perseverance; she's not stubborn."

Aunt Ruth always did see the best in her. Even more than her gram did. But that wasn't really saying much.

"If you don't want to fight, you shouldn't have started one. You threatened to pee on my seat. What are you, two?" Jeff spit the words out, sounding like the jerk her best friend always said he was.

After Kylie had ODed, she hadn't had anyone else that she could call best friend. Unless she wanted to count Jeff. She wanted him to be her best friend. She heard that married couples should be each other's best friends, but Jeff wasn't exactly kind and compassionate the way Kylie was.

'Course, Kylie had gotten hooked on drugs, and toward the end, the only thing she cared about was making money so she could buy her next fix. So yeah, she'd stolen Skyler's stash that she had under her mattress from working at the diner outside of Chicago.

She could hardly be mad at Kylie, since shortly after she'd stolen the money and Skyler had figured it out and confronted her with that, Kylie had ODed. And she was planning Kylie's funeral, not that it was much of a funeral.

She had never known how expensive it was to bury someone. Actually, it was cheaper to be cremated, so...she wasn't sure what Kylie's wishes were, but her friend had been cremated because that had been all Skyler could afford.

They'd had a little ceremony at the funeral home, although it was just Skyler and a couple other people from the diner who came.

She didn't know where Kylie's family was. Kylie never talked about them.

Kind of the way Skyler didn't really talk about her family either.

But she was going to turn over a new leaf and have a different life for her baby. Jeff was a respectable man with a steady job at Thompson's Trash and Recycling. He got up every morning at four o'clock and rode the garbage truck route around Chicago.

It was a hard job, but it paid well, and Jeff was a very dependable employee.

Of course, when he got off work on Friday afternoon, he was pretty much drunk from two hours later until the early hours of Sunday morning, but that's probably what she would do too if she had such a strenuous, difficult job.

"I won't pee on your seat. But I really do have to go. Please?"

"Fine. Whatever the next exit is, we'll take it. That's where you'll pee. Although, if you want to, I can stop along the road."

"No! I couldn't possibly go to the bathroom along the road. Someone might see me."

"It's not like they care. You're as big as a whale."

"That's why I need to pee all the time."

Jeff used to tell her she was the most gorgeous woman in the world. After a couple of beers, he acted like she was too.

Tears pricked her eyes, and she swallowed hard to push them away. Normal people were as big as a whale when they were pregnant. She was normal. And it wasn't completely abnormal for the father of the baby to look at a mother's pregnant body and not think she was sexy anymore.

Of course, she didn't really know how men thought, but they seemed to be attracted to the skinny girls. She'd always been skinny.

And she would be again, once the baby was born.

Lord, please let the next exit be soon. I don't think I can hold it too much longer.

She gritted her teeth against the pain as the baby moved and seemed to use her bladder as a trampoline, like it didn't already hurt the way it was lying on her.

If you were here, little guy, I would teach you where you're not allowed to sit, and that's on Mom's bladder.

She was going to teach her child everything she had been taught. Maybe she'd even take him to church. Gram had taken her once in a while, but by the time she'd gone to live at her grandma's house, she had been too big to think that there was much use in church.

At least she'd gone to school. She had her high school diploma. That was more than Kylie had. Still, because of Skyler's good recommendation, the diner had hired Kylie. Or maybe it was just a shortage of workers. Seemed like they were always short-staffed and she was having to pick up extra shifts, especially on the weekend, which made Jeff mad.

She wasn't sure what she was going to do when the baby was born. She didn't have maternity leave, so she'd have to take off, but she wouldn't be paid for it. And they depended on her salary to buy groceries, especially Jeff's alcohol. It took everything he made to pay the rent on their small apartment.

"Have you thought about names?" she asked and then cringed. She shouldn't have, because Jeff got upset when she talked about the baby.

"I don't care what you name the stupid rug rat." He gave her a look that made her want to crawl into herself. "I wasn't the one who got knocked up to begin with."

She didn't say anything. She'd tried to explain to him that she'd taken her birth control pills exactly the way she was supposed to, and she hadn't missed even one. But he hadn't believed her. He said that never happened with any of his other girlfriends, and he acted like she betrayed him somehow. Like she'd chosen to get pregnant.

Of course, she didn't really mind that she was, because she had a baby to give all of her love to. And someone to love her as well.

She never really had that.

"And I'm looking forward to having some time together so we can work on our relationship."

"Our relationship doesn't need any work. At least not on my end. You need to shove that brat out and get your figure back. That's the only thing that's wrong with our relationship."

"Oh, I'm sure it won't take any time at all to get back into shape." She tried to project confidence, although she'd heard that some people had a lot of trouble getting back into shape. "When you talk like that, it makes me feel like you're only interested in my body. And that you don't really care about me as a person or about my emotions—"

"I care about your emotions. Just not when you're a whiny, complaining mess. No one could put up with that kind of crap the way I have."

It was true, she had been more emotional when she was pregnant.

"Oh my goodness. My back hurts so bad." She put a hand behind her back, at the spot where it felt like her muscles were being torn apart.

"See what I mean? All you ever do is complain. 'I have to pee. My back hurts.'" He mimicked her voice in a whiny tone. "When are you going to grow up?"

"And why don't you grow a little compassion? You don't need to be a jerk all the time. You don't have a human growing inside of your body, jumping on top of your bladder, making every muscle in your body ache, and then your boyfriend has to go and be in a grumpy mood all the time and complain because I don't look the way I did when we first started dating. You were there too. I didn't make this baby on my own."

It felt good to yell at him. She always tried to get along, and she hardly ever gave him a piece of her mind until she just couldn't hold it in anymore. He had been a jerk the whole trip, like he didn't really want to get away. It was true, they really couldn't afford it, but who knew when they would ever have a chance to do it again. She... She wanted a honeymoon. Something romantic and sweet. Where Jeff smiled and treated her like a queen and she did everything in her power to make his life happier and easier and they lived together and grew old together, but they needed couple time in order to grow that strong bond.

"If you yell at me, I'm not stopping for you. So I guess if you want to pee, you'd better be nice. There you go with your whining, bawling, and complaining all the time. I'm never good enough. If I'm not good enough, go find some other sugar daddy to suck from."

Her hand squeezed into a fist, but she tried to force herself to relax and open it back up. He didn't mean it. He was tired and grumpy. They'd been on the road for several hours since breakfast, and in order to save money, they agreed they weren't going to stop for fast food but would stop at a grocery store and grab some groceries before they camped out along Lake Michigan.

She swallowed, feeling the desire to cry again, and pushed it back. She could handle this. She could be nice, even when he was mean. She did remember that much from Sunday school. It was supposed to magically make everyone love her. She wanted Jeff to love her.

"I'm sorry. I love you, Jeff." She looked over, trying to give him a tremulous smile, but he just stared at her.

"If you loved me, you wouldn't be such a witch all the time."

She wanted to give him a piece of her mind, but instead, she said, "You're right. I'll try to be nice and try not to complain anymore."

"It's too late to stop. And your apology isn't good enough. You're gonna have to show me how sorry you are."

A sign that said "Raspberry Ridge - two miles" flew by as Jeff angrily grasped the wheel, speeding up like they weren't already going fifteen miles an hour over the speed limit.

Everything would be okay. They'd stop. He'd grab something to eat. They'd be fine. He wouldn't be grumpy anymore, and she wouldn't have to pee for at least another hour or two.

She wouldn't drink anything. That would help. She hadn't been drinking anything, though. Maybe she was a little dehydrated, because she had a headache. It had started thumping behind her eyes, and now it crisscrossed her forehead.

She didn't say anything when he jerked the wheel, hitting the exit at highway speed, and didn't start braking until they were almost at the stop sign.

Sign up for Jessie's newsletter! Get a free book, access to exclusive bonus content, get fun and funny updates on her life on the farm and more!

A Gift from Jessie

View this code through your smart phone camera to be taken to a page where you can download a FREE ebook when you sign up to get updates from Jessie Gussman! Find out why people say, "Jessie's is the only newsletter I open and read" and "You make my day brighter. Love, love, love reading your newsletters. I don't know where you find time to write books. You are so busy living life. A true blessing." and "I know from now on that I can't be drinking my morning coffee while reading your newsletter – I laughed so hard I sprayed it out all over the table!"

Claim your free book from Jessie!

www.ingramcontent.com/pod-product-compliance
Lightning Source LLC
Chambersburg PA
CBHW020656010826
48969CB00013B/2071